DEE SNIDER'S
STRANGELAND

THE OFFICIAL NOVELIZATION BY
CHRISTIAN FRANCIS & DEE SNIDER

BASED ON THE SCREENPLAY BY
DEE SNIDER

Foreword

by Dee Snider

The movie was to be my next masterstroke. I reinvented the horror movie genre, created the first film rated R for scenes of torture (*you're welcome*) and created a terrifying new horror icon. The feedback to my script was amazing. After reading it my wife, Suzette was ready to divorce me ("*Who the fuck am I married to!?*"), my agent couldn't look me straight in the eye ("*You're...that guy!*") and I was getting accolades from all sorts of people in the horror industry (Tom Savini: "*Creepy man. Real creepy.*") I knew I was onto something special and when I found an indie studio not only ready to make my movie, but to let me star in it, I thought I was off to the races with a whole new career. *If only...*

The film production ran into terrible problems with the director (He Who Shall Not Be Named) and it was a real struggle just to get the film into some kind of reasonable shape for release. But with the love and support of an incredible editor (Jeff Kushner), co-producer (Dave Bushell) and film company (the late Shooting Gallery) I was ready to spew my perverse vision (my nightmares, not my dreams) onto an unsuspecting world. *Thud.*

The theatrical release was unimpressive and for the most part the critics didn't get it ("*StrangeLand* writer Dee Snider should be forced to get a lobotomy!"). Even so, the Shooting Gallery believed in the movie's potential and greenlit a sequel. Yay! The next signs of life were the rentals. StrangeLand was a one of the most rented *and never returned* movies of it's time. Horror fans were getting into the whole "helpless and suffering" thing and unbeknownst to me young filmmakers were taking notice. Eli Roth and James Wan (who both bow down before me, "We're not worthy! We're not worthy!") saw the bold new world I had invented and created powerful moneymaking franchises that set them on new successful career paths. *If only I could say the same.*

Any energy *StrangeLand* had built in that first year or so was lost when The Shooting Gallery was indicted by the federal government for "cooking the books" and illegal investment strategies. All their properties were seized and I spent the next *seven years* and thousands of dollars fighting in courts to retain the creative rights to my creation. By the time I got control of my property (except for the original print which Lionsgate controls distribution of to this day) interest in a *StrangeLand* sequel had cooled. Though there have been several false starts over the last 25 plus years, "*StrangeLand: Disciple*" has never seen the light of day. *And boy is it dark!* With all the torture films that have come out since it's inglorious release in 1997, I had to work really hard to lower the bar and create something that would say, "Captain Howdy is the father of all you fuckers and he's taking you to school!" But as of now, I have no takers. Sure, we've had three sequels of "Attack of the Killer Tomatoes" (and an animated series) but I can't get StrangeLand 2 made. Go figure.

But the cult status of my movie continues to grow. I make regular appearances at horror cons signing Captain Howdy photos ("Are we *ever* gonna get a sequel?") and get endless accolades for my sick creation. It's nice. *Frustrating, but nice.*

And now there's this. A legitimate, talented writer, Christian Francis has written a novelization of my movie and it's good. *Really good.* When Chris first approached me with the idea, he spoke of how visual the screenplay was. It had to be. I was creating a bold new world of horror and I needed the script reader to be able to really see exactly what I say in their minds eye. This lent itself to the novelization (and it the reason I'm the co-writer of this fine book) and allowed Chris to really take my corrupt vision to a whole other level. Thank you for that Chris. It means the world to me that people can now enjoy it in this format. And who knows? Maybe people with respond to *StrangeLand* in book form and we'll release "*StrangeLand: Disciple*" as a novel? Then maybe a studio will buy the IP and finally produce my fucking sequel! *One can dream, can't one?*

Dee Snider, September 2025

CHAPTER 1

STRANGERS IN THE NIGHT

HELVERTOWN, COLORADO, 1997

The calligraphy pen moved carefully and deliberately, dragging a smooth black trail across the granular rice paper. Its strokes were tight and controlled, forming sharp angular shapes that curled and hooked in symmetrical, tribal patterns. The hand that gripped the pen never paused, never trembled. Each line drawn was expert in its design, without a single mark out of place. There was ritual in these movements that carried an obsessive attention to detail.

The hand that held the pen could hear its own heartbeat, where each thump was part of a rhythm guiding the ink as they became lost in their creation.

Finally, the pen was lowered, and all attention was moved to the other side of the desk.

Slicing through the silence of the murkily lit room,

a sharp electronic shriek sounded. It was the cackling noise of a modem connecting. A frenetic mechanical scream of *bleeps* and *bloops* that ground itself in a signal.

The noises carried on, layer upon layer, until finally dropping away.

As they did, the computer screen came to life.

`Connecting.`
`Welcome to U.S.A. Online.`

The new pale glow lit up the room. On the monitor, various icons started to appear. As the cursor blinked to life, the hand guiding the mouse moved it across the screen, pausing over an icon labeled `People Connection` before clicking on it.

A deep voice began to hum. A slow, haunting rendition of *Strangers in the Night*, where each note was elongated uncomfortably.

The cursor continued to move as it selected an empty box: `Search Member Directory`.

As the box sat, waiting for input, two long, bony hands hovered over the keyboard. Gloved in black surgical latex, they began to type slowly.

`Female. Helvertown, CO.`
`Student . . .`

The man continued humming quietly as he typed the last search word: `Fun`.

The computer processed slowly, then populated the screen with a list of usernames alongside the real names.

The count read: `Items 1-20 of 34 matching criteria.`

The cursor clicked on the first name.

A member profile opened:

```
Screen name: Gru V Gal
Birth date: 8/3/78
Hobbies: Music, partying,
having fun
```

"Mmm," the man murmured, interested, as he stopped humming his song.

A click saved the profile to his address book, and `Gru V Gal` disappeared from the list.

The cursor slowly moved to the second name: `Piscese1313`. Another profile loaded.

```
Birth date: 9/28/42
Hobbies: Practicing for grandbaby
```

"Urgh," the man grumbled, less impressed. The profile was dismissed from the list as the cursor pressed on the red X at the end of the name.

Then the third: `MissXXX151`.

Their profile window opened.

```
Birth date: 9/5/82
Quote: Wine me, dine me, etc.
```

A long pause. The man stared at the screen with interest. His moan was almost inaudible but lustful as his eyes widened at the words on the screen.

That name was added to the address book without question.

He opened another window: `Locate a Member Online.`

The blank search field opened.

The fingers typed in: `MissXXX151`

Return.

The response came instantly.

```
MissXXX151 is in Teen Chat 3 in
People Connection.
```

The man chuckled with satisfaction.

The cursor moved to the menu bar and clicked `Departments` then `Rooms`.

A new window opened. `Active Public Rooms.` The list scrolled fast, the names of the chatrooms, flashing by one after the other.

```
Best Lil' Chat House
Lesbian Corner
Teen Flirts
Trekkies 2
Teen Chat 3
```

Click.
His cursor stopped.

You have just joined Teen Chat 3.

At the top of the user list, a new username appeared, his name: CaptHowdy.

Other usernames followed as the chat messages scrolled up rapidly:

Chevy9472: is that so
Pumkin4321: hi everyone!!!!!!!!!
BreakX007: why?
Minifin777: gravity sucks
Clown1313: Any Ladies 17+ in here?
BallboySSS: LIFE SUCKS

The cursor hovered over one name as a message appeared in the room:

MissXXX151: Hey, everyone.

The gloved hands began to type, each keystroke slow and deliberate, as the man took immense satisfaction from every movement.

A final, almost sensual press of the return button sent the message shooting through unseen phone lines. Coded as binary ones and zeros, it rushed through wires and routers faster than the speed of sound. It left the man's computer and hurtled across the other side of Helvertown.

It found MissXXX151 as the message popped up on her screen.

CaptHowdy: Hi MissXXX howzit going.

Genevieve Gage's bedroom was a mess of color, clutter, and angst. Posters covered the walls, rappers, rockers, and shirtless celebrities, with images ripped from glossy magazines, tacked at all angles. A typical middle-class fifteen-year-old girl's room. A girl who rebelled against anything she could whenever she could. Not out of need but out of boredom. With dark eyes, darker eyeliner, and long, straight black hair that she flipped out of her eyes constantly, she was a deliberate social misfit. She *chose* to be and would have it no other way.

A hi-fi stereo sat on a table under the windowsill, pumping out its music with heavy bass and shrieking guitars. On top of the drawers, the mirror that leaned against the wall was littered with Polaroids stuck to the rim, images of her and her friends, each with expressions of forced disillusionment. In front of the mirror, open makeup containers had been scattered across the top. All shades of black and red.

Wearing a black hoodie, Genevieve sat at her computer, cross-legged, on her worn-out desk chair, leaning forward as she stared at the screen.

Standing over her shoulder was her best friend, Tiana Moore. The same age but with a much more conservative style. Tiana wore fitted jeans, a long-sleeved crop top, and clean white sneakers. Her hair was thick and wavy, pulled back out of her face. She watched Genevieve with her arms crossed, looking at the screen in slight judgment, nowhere near as enamored with the chatrooms as Genevieve was.

"Here we go," Genevieve said, lighting up. "Check this guy out."

Tiana frowned, looking suspicious. "What kind of name is Captain Howdy anyway?"

Genevieve cracked her knuckles with a smile as she typed:

MissXXX151: Howdy Captain! *grin* What's the happs?

A response appeared almost immediately.

CaptHowdy: Nothin' much. Just hangin' out listening to some music. You like hip-hop?

Genevieve grinned. "I like this guy already." She typed back.

MissXXX151: I love it!!!!!! Which high school do you go to? Calhoun?

Another instant reply:

CaptHowdy: No, Kennedy. What you up to?

Genevieve typed faster.

Behind her, the song on the hi-fi ended, and the next track started. Tiana turned, the song piquing her attention way more than the chatroom had. She walked over, picked up the CD case, and checked the back.

"Damn, I love this song," she said. "When did you get this?"

Genevieve didn't look up. "Picked it up the other day."

Her fingers pressed the final key and sent the message.

MissXXX151: I'm hanging out with my girlfriend. Hey Capt, IM me.

Less than a minute passed before the system chimed again.

A message box popped open.

Somewhere down the internet lines, through the mess of electricity, a man with surgical gloves at his keyboard, staring at the screen, grinned as he continued to hum a song.

CaptHowdy: Want to come to a party?

Genevieve gasped, laughing into her hand. "Oh, I gotta go, right?"

Tiana's eyebrows shot up as she walked back over and read the message on the screen. "Let me get this straight," she said. "You're wanna go on a blind date with a screen name? Who is this guy?"

Genevieve grinned. "It's what's gonna happen to us all. We'll each have digital love stories. You'll meet, marry, and have cyber kids with the guy of your dreams, all totally online. As for me and Howdy . . . We'll live happily ever after in a virtual village somewhere in a suburban corner of the World Wide Web."

Tiana groaned.

Genevieve clicked through the menu bar and opened a profile search. "Everything I need to know about this guy . . . is right here." She typed in the username and hit the return key.

```
Member name: Randy Williams
Location: Helvertown, CO
Birth date: 9/16/78
Occupation: Duh... student
Quote: Hey bud, where's the
kegger?
```

Genevieve looked smug. "Feel better?"

Tiana hesitated, unsure. "I guess so."

Genevieve shrugged. "Hey, he didn't invite you," she said teasingly. "So, if it goes bad, it'll only be me who gets murdered. Sound good?"

"Gen, your dad's a detective. You should know better than this. And what about your mom? She wouldn't be fine with you going anywhere alone. Would she?"

Genevieve's smile faded as she sighed. The mention of her parents killed her buzz. She turned away from the keyboard and up at her friend. "I don't want to argue about this, okay? Let's just drop it."

"What? What's the matter? We're not arguing."

Genevieve sighed. She nodded. "Sorry, my bad . . . Just my folks . . . All they do is argue. Argue. Argue. Nonstop. And it always starts like this. With a small thing . . . And what's it all got them?" She paused, trying to not let the subject get the better of her. "Well, they've been talking about getting a divorce . . . And I don't want the same to happen to us."

"Oh, trust me, Gen, I'll never leave you," Tiana smiled. She then motioned to the computer. "So, how about we both go to this party? Huh?"

Genevieve blinked, surprised, pulled back from any negative emotion. "Tiana? At a party? Who *are* you? What alien has taken over your body?" She grabbed her friend's arms and gave her a playful shake. "What have you done with my friend?"

They both laughed.

Genevieve turned back to the screen and typed:

MissXXX151: Where? When? I'm bringing a friend, cool?

They stared at the monitor in silence.
A moment later, the chime sounded.

CaptHowdy: Tonight! 9pm! My house!

```
My parents are gone!!! HELL YES
YOUR FRIEND CAN COME!!!! It'll be
an awesome fun night!
```

The girls squealed in unison.

Tiana forgot her doubt in an instant.

"Get his address!" she yelled.

Genevieve's fingers flew over the keyboard, typing as fast as she could.

———

At the intersection off the freeway, a sign stood at the side of the road. Its reflective paint caught in the headlights of cars that entered the city limits.

Welcome to Helvertown, U.S.A.
A nice place to visit; a better place to live.
Population: 36,114
Town Supervisor: Richard K. Brantley
Founded: 1889

The rain fell in steady sheets over the main drag, washing the colors out of the town the heavier it got. Making the evening that much darker. Helvertown was just like any other American suburbia. With similar-looking houses. Similar-looking shops. Similar-looking people. It all had a quaint and wholesome veneer.

The streets were mostly empty. Being the quiet place it was, no shops were ever open past 6 p.m. The evening brought a close to commerce. All except for the liquor, porn and pawn establishments, that stayed open till the break of day.

Farther down the road, through the curtains of rain, past the rail tracks and into one of the affluent areas, stood a large house. A stately colonial-style home on Harrow Street, set back on a wide, carefully maintained lot. With a low hedge that bordered the front lawn, it was all trimmed expertly. Through a picket fence gate, the path to the house was lined with flowers that bent from the relentless downpour and up to a porch with a welcoming light. This house looked picture-perfect and well-loved.

Somewhere nearby, a dog barked and would not stop, barking at the rain as if it were an encroaching enemy . . . or sensing what was happening in the colonial-style house.

The front door flew open, slamming against the porch wall.

From the darkness, someone came running out. Desperate, barefoot, and screaming.

She stumbled down the steps, wild-eyed and gasping for air, as she bolted straight across the lawn. Her clothes were quickly soaked, and her hair was plastered to her face, washing away the streaks of blood all over her.

It was Genevieve Gage. She was running and not looking back, crying and screaming.

From behind, a shape barreled out after her. Much larger and much faster. Getting closer.

The rain had started to fall harder and louder. Soaking the ground in increasing torrents as it masked her cries.

Getting to the edge of the lawn, Genevieve slipped as her foot caught a plant. She managed to keep her balance and scramble onto the path. Her feet sharply slapped the stone as her fingers clawed ahead, trying to pull herself to freedom. Her breath tore out of her in panicked shrieks. Her fear was beyond anything she had ever felt before.

She desperately tried to will herself to go faster, but her desperation got the better of her, and her foot slid again. This time, she was unable to correct as she fell and landed hard on the ground, scraping her hands and knees on impact, only a few feet from the sidewalk.

Behind her, the shape could have caught up to her already but instead had slowed and was taking its time. Watching her fall with glee.

She tried to scream again, but the breath was knocked out of her as the shape pounced.

Her hands clawed at the slick concrete in front of her, scratching at the path, trying to pull away. And as she did, one of her fingernails bent and snapped. She would have cried out in pain, but her adrenaline overrode everything. She tried to—

A gloved hand closed around her ankle, yanking her onto the grass.

"No!" Genevieve cried.

The shape quickly moved above her, as its muscular arm swung something heavy through the air.

The object struck the back of Genevieve's head with a wet *thunk*.

Her body seized, then collapsed, hitting the cold path. Her eyes were half open and empty as blood pooled beneath her temple, dark and thick, smearing on the grass in the rain.

Her legs twitched.

She was then pulled back. The attacker, the shape, dragged her limp body back to the house. Her head bumped against each step on the way up the stoop. Her hair matting thicker with blood as it seeped out of her.

The shape hummed as it moved. A slow, ominous version of *Strangers in the Night*.

The yard fell still once more. The rain rinsed away all traces of the attack, one streak at a time, aside from the one fingernail, snapped and on the path.

Somewhere, the dog was still barking into the stormy night.

———

The next morning was gray and cold. The rain had stopped, but the sky remained heavy and oppressive. Inside the Gage household, at the small dining table off from the kitchen, Detective Mike Gage sat in a shirt and tie. He was rereading his notes on a yellow legal pad, trying to decipher his own handwriting.

Mike was in his early forties, in shape, but exhausted, and his face did not hide that fact.

On the table in front of him, a pot of coffee and a

full mug lay cold, after being forgotten about for the last hour. He was too embroiled in his work.

Picking up a pencil, he added a few words to the pad. He stopped halfway as he stared at the wall, thought some more, then quickly crossed out what was just written.

This was getting nowhere.

Finally noticing the coffee, he picked up the mug and took an unwelcome sip of cold, black liquid. He grimaced in annoyance. But this was familiar, as he always forgot.

A cabinet slammed in the kitchen behind him.

Mike didn't flinch.

Toni Gage, his wife, stomped through the adjoining room, still in her dressing robe, hair wild and unbrushed. She was more Italian than American in temperament, and even just out of bed, she carried herself with frustration. Her every move was loud: the way she opened the cabinet, the way she filled the kettle. She didn't look into the dining room, but every step and slam she made was deliberate and meant to be heard by him.

Mike stood and walked over to his briefcase, grabbed a folder from it, and pulled out a wad of large photographs. Laying them on the dining table, he closely studied each. They were of crime scenes. Graphic, autopsy-level. Close-up images of bloody wounds and missing limbs.

As he scrutinized them, he did not notice Toni walk in. She peered down at the horror in the images and, without a word, walked back out with a look of disgust on her face.

Mike pretended not to notice as he sat at the table and started to reread his notes, checking specific photos.

He did not know if ten seconds or ten minutes had passed when his name was screamed from upstairs.

"*MIKE!*" came his wife's angry summons, echoing through the house.

Toni was standing in Genevieve's bedroom, looking unimpressed. She glanced at the still-made bed, then to the mess on the floor. Her teeth clenched as she picked up a shirt and a pair of jeans and placed them on a nearby chair.

"*MIKE!*"

She heard his reluctant stomping up the stairs, then down the hallway toward her.

"Yeah?" he asked begrudgingly as he appeared in the doorway.

Toni glared. "Notice anything, do you?"

Confused, he glanced around the room briefly. "What exactly am I supposed to be looking for?"

She rolled her eyes, as if that was the dumbest question imaginable. "Everyone, be impressed. We have ourselves the world's greatest detective right here," she snapped sarcastically before motioning around the room. "Your daughter?"

He raised an eyebrow.

"Five foot two?" she continued. "God, Mike . . . She didn't come home last night! What is wrong with you?"

He paused. Looking around the room again. "So, where is she?"

"She went out with Tiana. I bet she spent the night at her house, even though I told her that if she hadn't been back by ten"—she pointed at Mike as if it were his fault—"I'm going to kill her for not calling us."

From another room, the phone rang.

Shaking her head, Toni left the room, mumbling as she stomped, "See if you can remember what she looks like."

Mike shrugged. He walked farther into the room, not knowing what he was looking for. As he absentmindedly bumped the desk chair, it nudged the desk, which moved the computer mouse.

BEEP-BEEP-BEEP.

The computer woke from its sleep mode, and its screen lit up.

The words *U.S.A. Online* slowly appeared.

Mike frowned. Looking down at the keyboard, he tapped a few keys, having zero idea what he was doing. The computer beeped angrily. Shrill tones that proved his inexperience. He pressed another button. Another beep. Then another. His annoyance with the computer came out in a grunt as he slammed his hand down on the keyboard, which let loose a collection of simultaneous beeps.

The computer was still on, facing him with the same message of welcome.

In exasperation, he reached behind the desk, found the power cord, and yanked it out of the wall.

The screen went black.

A small, pointless victory that made him smile.

Turning, his thoughts returned to his case downstairs, to the crime scene photos. He almost jumped when he saw Toni had come back, standing in the doorway and staring at him. The antagonism had evaporated from her. She just looked pale and shocked as she stared.

"What is it?" he asked.

"That was Tiana's mother," she replied quietly. "She didn't go home. Nor did Gen."

Mike's expression didn't change, but his voice lowered. "Toni, they're all right, okay? It's Gen. She knows what she's doing. Call her friends if it'll make you feel better."

He stepped closer and put a reassuring hand on her arm. "She probably forgot to call, that's all. Probably went to a party and is waking up with one hell of a hangover."

"She's fifteen!" Toni barked.

"And? What were *we* doing at fifteen?"

She did not reply. She did not have to. In his mind, he had made his point. With a smile, he walked by her and into the hallway. "I'm late for a lineup," he said, not looking back as he walked toward the stairs. "Don't worry. She'll be fine."

Toni didn't move. "Yeah? Well, I'm not."

As Mike left, she exhaled loudly. Wondering. Worrying.

———

The apartment was nothing more than a bachelor's cave. Sparse. Functional, and a space that never expected or wanted company. Everything important here lived within arm's reach. Beyond the carpeted living room, a narrow eat-in kitchen was divided by a small countertop that had seen way more takeouts than home cooking. And the cooking that did happen was more from a packet than prepared from scratch. The oven sat, unused, whereas the microwave was well-worn and food-stained within.

A tall black entertainment center sat on the far side of the living room. With a huge television, it was bracketed by a high-end hi-fi on one side and a neatly filed collection of videocassettes and compact discs on the other. On the shelves sat trophies from a more involved past, as well as photos of a guy who once knew how to live in the now, frozen mid-laugh or mid-flex.

The television was on, flashing a chaotic music video across its pixels, but the volume was turned down to zero. Instead, the radio on the hi-fi filled the room with the sterile tones of the *News at Noon* broadcast. Weather. Traffic. Another crime. Another sad day of reporting.

From the bedroom door, Detective Steve Christian

walked out, half-dressed, holding a cordless phone to his ear, grinning like his punchline had already landed.

"Softball? Real men don't play softball, dude. There's no bodychecking."

He laughed, nodding as he listened to the person on the other end of the line. "Righty-o. Later, bud."

The call ended with a click, and Steve dropped the phone back in the cradle on the sideboard. He walked on autopilot into the kitchen, opened a cabinet, and poured himself a big bowl of Cap'n Crunch that could feed a family.

He walked back into the living room, spooning mouthfuls of cereal in one after another as he watched to the fast cuts of the silent music video. A smile spread across his face as he reached for the remote and increased the volume. The bland news report clicked away as the music filled the room like a wall of noise.

Steve didn't flinch. Still chewing, he put the cereal on the table and grabbed his police issues revolver from its holster, then moved back to the sofa. He didn't rush. This was all part of his routine. Something he did each morning. Breakfast, music, gun.

With the bowl in reaching distance, he popped the weapon's cylinder and checked the rounds. As he inspected the barrel, his chewing never stopped, but if it got close, he leaned forward and spooned another mouthful in.

Even though he was lost in what he was doing, a buzzing on his belt broke his momentum. It didn't make a noise but instead vibrated into his side. His pager.

Wiping his lips with the back of his hand, he grabbed the pager and glanced at the message. His expression dropped as he read the words.

Immediately, he hit the power button on the remote. The television and hi-fi turned off in unison. The revolver went back into its holster and was strapped around his shoulders. The cereal bowl was left on the table.

———

A burst of white-hot, blinding flame broke through the poorly lit room. The hiss of a welding torch screamed out, and sparks shot outward, bouncing off the shadowed concrete below.

Through the narrow slits of a welding mask, a man watched as his large, gloved hands gripped the metal.

The final weld soon sparked, finishing off his work with a confident flourish.

The torch then hissed off as steam began to rise from the cooling metal.

The gloved hands tested their work, a new hinge on a metal ring. A ring the size of a human neck. They opened the ring up, then snapped it shut again.

The hands then held it up to the light for closer inspection.

The man behind the mask said nothing.

But he was smiling.

———

The buzz of old fluorescent strip lighting and the sickly smell of sugar clung to the inside of the convenience store. Two uniformed officers stood near the counter next to a jittery employee holding a cup of steaming coffee as she tried to regain her composure. Her eyes stared ahead, just beyond the rack of discounted chips and off-brand soda, down to where a pair of lifeless legs protruded from the aisle. Blood pooled around this body and spread across the linoleum into her line of sight. She was unable to look away as the officers asked their questions once again to her.

On the other side of the small store, Detective Gage was crouched next to another employee no older than twenty, who sat on the floor in a state of shock. With a blood trail drying down the right side of his face, the wound on his scalp had already begun to clot. A paramedic stood to his other side, tending to the gash with a usual grim detachment.

". . . And you've never seen this guy before?" Mike asked, knowing these questions would not amount to much.

The kid winced as the paramedic dabbed his wound. He shook his head slowly, careful not to move too much in a state of obvious discomfort.

As Mike's phone rang from his pocket, it made the kid jump.

Mike motioned to the paramedic. "Give him something for the pain, would ya?" he said, reaching for his phone.

Standing, he stepped away down the aisle as he answered. "Detective Gage?"

"Have you found out anything yet?" Toni's voice said as it came through the speaker, thin and trembling. She was imagining the worst and too worried to be praying for the best.

"Toni?" he replied, not surprised at her calling for the third time since he started his shift. He paused, consciously trying—and failing—to hide his annoyance. "No. Nothing's changed since the last time you called."

He drifted toward the front of the store, turning his back to the body on the floor, to the blood, to the shell-shocked employees.

"Look, I'm still waiting to hear back from state and local."

"That was over six hours ago," Toni shot back. "I'm going out of my mind here, Mike."

Mike rubbed his brow as he mentally forced himself not to react. "Toni, please, Just try to re—"

"Where are you now?"

Mike hesitated as he looked around at the store. "Now? I'm on a call. I can't just stay at my desk."

There was silence. Then a sharp reply.

"Un-fucking-believable."

Mike's patience was increasingly thinning, as was his wife's. "And you sure you didn't say something to set her off? You know how she can be." He knew he should not have said anything. He knew what the reaction would be. But like their whole marriage was now, arguments and anger were the standard.

"Oh, that's what you think? That it couldn't possibly be something YOU said?" Toni shouted. "You don't even talk to her. You never make time for her. EVER."

Mike glanced at the paramedics, at the officers, and at the red-and-blue flickering lights outside the window. He needed this conversation to stop. He tried to sound calm, but it came out snide. "Toni. You know we gotta wait forty-eight hours—"

"Wait? WAIT?" she snapped back. "It's your damn daughter, for God's sake. Don't give me that bullshit. You're a fucking DETECTIVE. Make something happen!"

With that, the line went dead.

Mike stared at his phone as if it might come back to life at any moment, and if she did, he promised himself that he would say sorry for speaking to her like that. But it didn't, and part of him knew it wouldn't. Maybe when they were first together, a quick apology would be offered at the first opportunity. Not now.

With a sigh, he slid the phone back into his pocket and turned back to the crime scene. Business was resumed as he pushed his emotions as far down as he could. Switching it all off to carry on investigating a dead body.

"How's his head?" he asked, walking over to the paramedic.

Before the man could answer, a nervous voice spoke up from behind him.

"Ex-Excuse me, Detective Gage?"

Mike turned as an officer stepped forward, stiff-backed and youthful. Officer Jarmel, wearing a uniform ironed with precision, had not been out of the academy for more than a year but looked like he hadn't slept in two. The constant parade of blood and violence had waned any exuberance he once had for the job.

"You've got a message from the precinct," he said.

Mike stared back, waiting.

Jarmel was intimidated by Mike, as were most of the young officers, and lost focus for a second.

"Well," Mike said, "are you going to tell me or stand there, starin' all day?"

"Oh. Yeah. Sure. Sorry, sir," Jarmel said. He glanced at his notebook, reading the words aloud. Not thinking about what he was saying. "There was a report that came into Detective Christian. He asked that I let you know. Known S.O. currently on parole. Witness reports of subject entering residence with a young female, matching description of one Genevieve Gage."

Mike stomach felt like it fell a hundred feet down. "S.O.?" he asked rhetorically, knowing exactly what it meant but hoping he heard wrong.

Jarmel continued, "Yes, sir, it means sex offender." The officer's voice suddenly faded as he realized what he had just said. He hadn't pieced it together as he took the notes and came in here with the message. Genevieve

Gage. Detective Gage. "Oh no . . . She . . . she's your daughter?"

The blood drained from Mike's face, but he didn't say a word. He just turned and hurried for the door.

The words Toni had shouted down the phone to him still rang in his ears. *It's your damn daughter, for God's sake.*

CHAPTER 2

TRY NOT TO SPEAK

The office of Captain Churchill Robbins felt more like a private residence than a police office. Everything inside had been meticulously arranged. Framed commendations and photographs lined the walls, interspersed with symbols of quiet discipline, Eastern Asian art prints, a framed black belt certificate, and a perfectly pruned bonsai tree resting on the windowsill. Alongside these emblems of serenity and order, between the photographs, hung a Silver Star, the medal he earned during his exemplary service in Vietnam.

On the wide mahogany desk sat a miniature zen garden, with sand delicately combed into spirals surrounding a single smooth stone. Captain Robbins sat in front of it, absentmindedly moving a miniature rake through the sand. As he did, he stared at the photo on his desk: a picture of his wife, two sons, and daughter. His peace.

He was a man who kept himself in shape out of habit with no vanity. He was trim, toned, gray-haired, and nothing about him was out of place. He may have been out of the military for years, but he still carried himself like a soldier. He was someone who didn't speak unless he had something to say, and when he did, people listened.

The officer door opened without a knock.

Detective Christian walked in. His shirt was still untucked since he left his apartment hours before.

"Captain," he said, "I just spoke to Tiana Moore's parents."

Robbins nodded in acknowledgment, not stopping as he combed the sand.

"They're a mess," Steve continued. "After what they told me, there's not a chance in hell she's a runaway." He took a second to breathe as the captain raised an eyebrow. "Well, I mean, that's what I believe. Not that I'm an expert or anything. No parents believe their kids would run away, right?"

Robbins calmly set the small rake and rested his hand beside it. He looked up at Steve.

"What do you have?" he asked, straight to the point.

Steve thought about taking a seat but quickly reconsidered as he spoke. "High school honor roll. Student council. In the choir. Perfect attendance . . . And check this, she and Genevieve Gage even bought tickets to see a Psychotic Method concert *tomorrow night*."

He paused for effect.

"So, what's the chance before she runs away before that? Leaving the tickets in her room? For a band she has a poster of on the wall?"

Robbins leaned back in his chair, thinking. "Where's Gage?"

"He's on Ardmore. Robbery homicide in a 7-11. He got the call while we were still piecing things together. Should be out for a couple more hours."

Robbins' voice went lower as he caught a glance of his daughter in the photo. "If she was *my* daughter . . . I think I'm going to team you up with Morgan on this case," Robbins said instead.

"No way Gage sits this one out. He won't allow that."

The phone on Robbins's desk rang.

The captain picked it up. "Speak."

He listened as he furrowed his brow. Without a word, he extended the receiver to Steve, who hesitated before taking it.

"Hello?"

A beat of silence as he listened.

Then another.

His posture changed.

"Right . . ."

There was more said as Steve listened. His jaw clenching.

"That mother fu—" He started but caught himself, eyes flicking to his captain. "No, I'll take care of it. Right."

Steve handed the phone back and stood silently, needing to tell Robbins but not sure how.

"Just say it," Robbins sighed.

"I . . . fucked up, Cap," Steve finally admitted. "The call . . . It was . . . I've got a lead, you see . . . One . . . One of my regulars. Derek Murphy."

Robbins's expression soured even more. "I remember him well. Unfortunately. Pederast. Drug user. Unlawful imprisonment. Rape. Aggravated assault. Torture."

Steve nervously smirked. "Yeah, a real beautiful guy."

Robbins was already putting the pieces together as he saw there was more.

"You told Gage?" he prompted.

Steve nodded. "I got a message to him to let him know. But . . ."

"You didn't think he would drop everything to go over there?" Robbins shook his head. "Damnit, Steve. Get over there. *Now*. Gage will be ready to kill if he finds anything. What were you thinking?"

———

The third floor of the apartment hallway was dull in shadow as the late afternoon sun pressed through a small, dirty window at the end of the corridor. The carpet here was frayed at the edges and worn in its center, exposing the threads. Years of footsteps had drained the color and fabric from the once-decadent pattern. And this was not the kind of establishment that would update anything, even if no longer able to serve its purpose. Along the ragged carpet, all the way down the hallway, apartment doors lined either side. All of which were closed and locked. Full of people who could barely make ends meet, people freshly out of jail and people whose lives had not been that lucky.

Derek Murphy stood in front of one of the doors, his key jammed into the lock. His hands were skeletal, and he was a very twitchy man. From years of drug abuse, he was a shell of what he once was. He looked homeless, though he wasn't and smelled worse. Like stale urine stained into rancid meat. His hair was stringy, his jeans too large for him and sagging, and his breath was uneven and wheezing. He was a wreck.

"Derek Murphy!"

The call came from the end of the corridor, at the top of the stairwell.

Murphy's fear kicked in as he slowly turned, peering over his shoulder, expecting to see the worst.

The person standing down the corridor was silhouetted by the murky light dripping in through the window behind them. They were just a shape walking toward him.

Murphy spun the key and wrenched the door open, disappearing inside with a slam as the locks clacked frantically behind him.

"Derek Murphy!" the voice roared again.

. . .

Outside, the rain had stopped, but the alleyway still glistened with moisture. On the rear of the building, the fire escape sat crookedly, its old frame rusted around the bolts, only holding itself upright through happenstance more than any firm fixtures.

At the top, one of the third-floor windows had been painted shut over a decade ago and the view blocked up with newspaper that had been taped inside. But none of that could stop the crash of glass that burst outward, scattering shards across the fire escape. With it, Murphy had come exploding through, having been hurled outward with an incredible force.

He slammed into the metal grating of the escape, the impact jarring his body. But even so, he pushed through the pain, forcing himself upright. Without any hesitation, without a thought for his safety, he vaulted over the railing. All that was in his mind was a need to escape.

His fall was fast, and his landing was hard.

He came crashing down onto the roof of a parked car, feetfirst, crushing it inward. All the windows shattered under his weight. But Murphy did not stop. He rolled off the crumpled vehicle and, in terrible agony, limped toward the road, crying in pain. He could not stop. He could not let the agony searing through his body stop him from getting away.

High up, climbing out the broken third-floor window, Detective Christian moved with far more control but no less urgency. He stepped onto the fire escape, gun in hand, as his eyes locked onto Murphy in the alley below. He could see the man hobbling, pulling something from his pocket as he moved. Tiny plastic baggies that soon hit the ground, one after another. Evidence that was recklessly being ditched.

Steve didn't care about the drugs. He was not here for that. He took the steps three at a time until he got to the ground and gave chase.

In front of his squalid apartment building was a semi-commercial street. Low-end storefronts in dilapidated shells. The kind of street that felt somewhat abandoned even though it wasn't.

Murphy shot out between two parked cars, head low, mouth open, lungs painfully wheezing, and he tried to run. He barely made it across the street as Steve came thundering from behind, launching himself over the hood of the car and slamming into Murphy before he even knew what had hit him.

Both men crumpled as Their limbs tangled.

Murphy screamed as he landed on his hip. His pain increased exponentially.

"Goddamn!" he wailed. "You . . . *Fuck* . . . you hurt me!"

He writhed, tried to pull free, but Steve pinned him down.

Murphy persisted. "I been clean, man! Since I made parole! No kids, no nothin'! You gotta believe me!"

Steve, with the gun in hand, cold and sudden, drove the barrel into the bridge of Murphy's nose.

Everything froze, and it felt as like even the street held its breath.

Steve leaned down closer. His words were slow and pointed. "Where's the girl?" he asked.

Murphy's eyes widened as his voice cracked. "Girl? No way, I'm off that underage shit. I ain't touched a baldy in—"

Steve's expression twisted into a greater fury, and Murphy could see it.

"Wh-What are you doing?!" he cried, panic taking over.

"She's a detective's daughter," Steve seethed. "You son of a bitch."

The hammer of his gun clicked back.

Murphy sobbed. "Don't! Fuck! I'm not . . . *Shit*! I swear . . . Please!"

Tires screamed nearby, stealing Steve's attention to the dark, unmarked car that skidded into view, with rooftop police lights flashing silently.

As the car's brakes locked up, the driver's side door flew open. Mike Gage was already running as he got out.

"Hey!" he shouted. "What the hell's going on?"

Steve didn't move his gun.

"Not a problem, Gage," he said calmly. "Everything's under control."

"Whoa," Mike said, approaching slowly as he realized what was happening, hands out like he was calming a wild animal. "Come on. Not like this. He's not worth the bullshit I.A. investigation."

Before Steve could answer, another voice screamed into the scene.

"Get your fuckin' hands off my brother!"

A punch landed on Steve's back like a hammer.

Candy Murphy had come out of nowhere.

She then attacked Steve from behind, screaming and swinging. Steve stumbled off Murphy, totally caught off guard.

"Candy!" Murphy gasped from the floor. "Easy! Don't!"

Mike quickly moved in, grabbing Candy by the arms and pulling her off Steve.

She shrieked as she was held, thrashing with all of her might. "You already locked him up because some lying bitch yelled rape!" she screamed hatefully. "Haven't you fuckin' bastards done enough!?"

Mike dragged her a few steps farther. "It's over! Calm down."

"Yeah?" Candy spat her words. "Well, tell that asshole to keep his goddamn hands to himself! I got a lawyer with no conscience who would love to fuck you all six ways from Sunday!"

Steve stared at Candy. She was young, slim, with long dark hair. He then realized the mistake that had been made.

Murphy wiped his nose with his sleeve, still with a pained look of fear as he got to his feet. "I don't know nothin' about a kid," he said, half to Mike, half to no one. "I told you, I'm legit."

"Get the fuck out of my sight," Steve muttered as he holstered his weapon.

Murphy didn't wait for another chance. He moved

over to his sister, wheezing, then hurried away fast, disappearing into their apartment building.

Mike stood still, watching them go, before turning to his partner.

"What the fuck's going on? Putting a gun in his face? Shit, Steve!" he said. "Then you just let him *go*? Just like that? What about Gen? I got your message. What the fuck is this?"

Steve shrugged. "You saw that girl, right? You see how much she looked like Gen? She was the girl that witness saw him take into his apartment."

Mike thought as the reality sank in. "Yeah . . . *Fuck . . .*"

"And that's good news," Steve added. "Better she's *not* here, right? Better she's off partying it up than this?"

Mike nodded. Unable to argue the point. But he could not let go of what happened. He motioned to the spot in the street where Steve had his gun pointed at Murphy. "But you can't do it *that* way. You *gotta* stay cool, you understand? You gotta keep a clear head."

"You know what's funny," Steve chuckled. "Captain told me to get here before you in case *you* did something stupid. Like he never knew that, out of the two of us, it was you with the level head."

――――――

The next day, Robbins paced through the homicide division corridor toward the lobby. As he did, before he could look around, he was caught.

"Captain Robbins?" the voice of Lindsay Scott called out.

Lindsay was a beat reporter for the Helvertown Herald. Aged in his mid-thirties, he was eager and always in the building, always underfoot. He wore a sports coat over his too-neat shirt and khaki combo. A typical local reporter with no real experience, he hung around waiting for a story. And he was always hopeful. The cassette recorder he held always ran. Hoping to catch a soundbite. And right now, he pushed the recorder close to Robbins' face.

Robbins didn't break stride. He was used to this.

"Lindsay," he deadpanned.

"What can you tell me about the missing girls?"

Robbins kept walking across the lobby.

"Are any of the family's suspects?"

That one made Robbins pause for half a second before forcing himself to continue.

Lindsay continued. "I've seen the assault complaint lodged against Detective Christian by a Ms. Candy Murphy. Will he be suspended?"

Robbins let out a low, irritated sound as he vanished through the doorway into the detectives' bullpen.

Lindsay stopped in his tracks, his eyes fixed on the back of the door closing. A door stated: "NO PUBLIC ENTRY." His shoulders sagged, and his voice lost all energy as he lifted the recorder to his mouth.

"No comment," he said into the microphone quietly. He then clicked the stop button and mumbled again, "No goddamn comment."

. . .

Inside the detective's bullpen area, the desks told you everything you needed to know about the people who sat behind them.

Steve leaned back in his chair, a telephone headset on, scrolling through documents on his computer. He looked tired, but he worked like he always did, fast and direct.

Mike's desk was another story. It looked like it belonged to a man twenty years older than he was. No computer. No headset. Just stacks of paperwork next to a heavy typewriter that was older than most of the new cops on beat.

He also had a thick, heavy folder open on the desk. With a page full of mugshots, separated by crime. These faces stared back in black and white, and in the section he was looking at, each person photographed was a father's nightmare. He turned the pages slowly, glancing over each image in turn as well as the small amount of details below.

Behind him, footsteps approached.

"Gage?"

He didn't look up as Robbins came to stand beside the desk.

"I wanted to talk to you, Mike, in private."

"I'm okay," Mike replied, knowing exactly what his captain wanted to talk about.

Robbins spoke quieter. "You know we can make

arrangements to get you some time off if you need it? Especially after yesterday's mishap with Derek Murphy."

Mike nodded. "I've had better days. But I'm good right here."

Robbins nodded and then turned to Steve.

"As for you . . . Seems the press has wind of what you did yesterday."

Steve glanced up. "Boss, this is a police investigation, not a photo op. And we're talking about the daughter of one of our own. We gotta make a statement that no one can hide."

"No statements," Robbins replied sharply. "I want you to stop waving your gun around like it's your dick. We can't afford your stupidity to not only bring the department into disrepute but also ruin an active investigation."

The room went quiet as all the detectives listened.

"You're *both* too close to this, and we cannot afford errors," he continued. "Steve, you're too cocksure—and, Gage, it should not be your case. You shouldn't even be at work."

Mike protested, "I don't—"

"But," Robbins said, "I am glad you were there yesterday."

Steve rolled his eyes. "Aw, jeez, I was just scaring the guy. Not like he deserved anything less."

Robbins shook his head. "Tell me why I shouldn't just reassign Morgan and Baker to this case."

Mike stood. "Please, don't do that," he said. "We

can handle it just fine. And I know I can find her. Better than anyone here."

Steve stepped in beside him. "As for Morgan and Baker? What do they know about this kind of case anyway? They're robbery."

Mike stepped closer. "Church." He spoke quietly, using Robbins's first name, a card he rarely had the nerve to play. "She's my daughter. You gotta understand. I can do this."

Steve added, "Come on, Captain. You gotta believe me. I wasn't gonna shoot. I just needed to find her. I had to scare him."

"Okay, but you are partners. Remember that." He looked at Steve. "So, no more lone-wolf-kamikaze bullshit." Then he glared at Mike. "So, no doing anything alone . . . I want you two stitched at the hip. Yin and yang." He looked at them each in turn. "And the moment even one of you steps out of line, both of you are behind a desk. Understand? I know she's your daughter, Gage, but that cannot be at the expense of the law."

Dampness clung to the basement walls as the smell of smoke drifted around. This unfinished room was lit only by candles. Dozens of them. Set along the floor, on shelves, on whatever flat surface that could hold them. Their glow cast shadows across the bare cinder block and onto the hanging ductwork overhead. Nothing about this place suggested comfort. Nothing about it was meant to. It was designed to be cold. Designed to be devoid of emotion.

A pull-up bar had been bolted onto a beam on the ceiling, secured with large screws. Below it, a man stood. His arms stretched upward as his fingers gripped the bar.

He grabbed hold and lifted himself up, steady and slow. Then down. Then up again at a measured and controlled pace. His whole body was a taut frame of muscle and sinew. Lean and strong.

He did not speak.

He did not rush.

He took his time.

He did not even lose a breath.

It was easy for him, even when he felt the burn in each arm.

When he reached a silent count of one hundred, he dropped to the floor. His feet landed without sound, and he had not even broken a sweat.

Standing still, he enjoyed the moment. The throb in his sinews. The pulsing of his blood.

With that done, he turned and slowly walked up the narrow stairs. As he ascended, each step he took creaked as the wood groaned beneath his solid weight.

He passed through the doorway and into a long, narrow hallway. The floor was bare concrete and led to a pair of sliding wood-paneled doors.

He stopped closer. Inside, he could hear sounds. Muffled. Shifting. Something soft moving against something hard. Breathing. Whimpering. All faint but all pleasing to him.

Genevieve's eyes were closed. She was unconscious but not still.

Her head moved slightly but not on its own accord. Her body was being manually adjusted, lifted, shifted. She was being manipulated, arranged.

The man parted his lips, his black, tattoo-stained lips, which exposed a row of teeth, each sharpened, filed to points.

A voice came from behind the mouth. A voice laced with malice.

"There," he said. "That's better, right?"

Genevieve's eyes began to flutter, slowly at first, as her shallow breathing quickened. She wasn't aware of where she was or who she was in front of. But the fog in her mind was lifting. And as it did, awareness came back to her in pieces. The sound, the temperature, the dull ache in her limbs. The cold, hard surface beneath her. The memory of running down a path. The memory of falling.

She managed to move her head slightly, rocking it from side to side as she tried to force herself awake, but there was a thick haze upon her. She needed to focus, but everything in her was sluggish.

It may have been cold where she was, but her body was sweating. The back of her head stung . . . Her mouth stung. Everything felt . . . wrong.

She tried to speak. But what came out wasn't words. It was a sound, trapped.

She tensed as she forced her eyes to open wider, blinking rapidly as she fought against the tide of exhaustion that weighed upon her. Unsteady, yellow pinpricks of flame, the light from the candles around her, wavered in her vision. There were dozens of them here, all around the room.

She tried to move again, but something pulled against her wrists.

She wanted to scream, to cry to help. To call for her mom or dad. But when she finally summoned the strength, she realized . . . her mouth wouldn't open.

She tried again, harder. Her entire body strained with the effort. But her lips didn't part. Her throat hurt. Her lips hurt. The panic within her came in sharply as she felt the small dots that stung around her mouth. The dots that hurt when she moved her jaw even a fraction.

She then remembered her escape from that house. Of the thing that followed her . . . The large tattooed, pierced thing . . . Then the blackness that followed.

It was real. It had not been a nightmare.

She ran her tongue through her forced-closed mouth as best as she could. The tip ran across the dozen or so strands that ran vertically from her top to her bottom lip.

Thread. Thick, coarse. Pulled through her skin in tight little knots.

She could not fathom what had happened. How it happened.

She could not see that her mouth had been sewn shut. Cruelly. Terrifyingly. Every stitch holding her back from making a noise.

The cries she wanted to let out came as a muffled moan.

Her eyes began to fill with tears.

"Try not to speak," the man said, in a calming, almost caring tone.

CHAPTER 3

LAKESIDE

B y the time another day came, the sun held high over Helvertown yet was once more hidden behind endless stormy clouds. It was so gloomy outside, that the early morning felt like almost like evening.

Inside the police headquarters, the lobby was mostly empty for once. A few officers moved through, heads down, clutching their morning coffees and donuts, still in their sleepy fugues.

Steve entered through the front doors. Unlike most of the others coming on duty, he looked refreshed and ready to start another day.

Across the other side, he soon noticed Mike near the vending machine, not looking as well turned out as he was.

Standing rigid, Mike gripped a dollar bill as he stared at the blinking slot like it had just insulted him. He tried to put the money in once more, but the machine refused his bill and spat it back almost immediately.

Mike's eyes were heavy, and he wore the same clothes as the day before. It was not only obvious that he hadn't gone home and changed but also that he had not slept and stayed at his desk working all night.

"You want me to get that?" Steve said, walking up beside him.

"Fucking things," Mike said, feeling the exhaustion. "I just want a damn chocolate bar."

Steve took his bill, smoothed the edges, turned it and slid it into the slot. The machine accepted it on the first try.

Mike gave a humorless shake of his head. "Fuck you, Steve."

"Ah, you love me and know it," he joked in reply.

"You got the NCIC printout yet?" Mike asked, shifting back to work. But before Steve could respond, he kept going. "And please don't tell me you didn't phone in the request . . . They're not going to call *us*, you know? We're a local precinct in a town nobody can find on a map. You have to call them, or we're not gonna get shit!"

Steve raised a hand, silencing him with a smirk. "I called the damn FBI, okay?" he said. "The report could be on my desk. Who knows? I just walked in here. You see anyone come in and drop it off? As you obviously haven't left."

"No one came in." Mike inhaled deeply.

"You holding it together okay?"

Mike just looked at his partner wearily. "What do you think?"

Steve motioned to the coffee machine. "How do you take it?"

"Black."

"You sure you don't want decaf?"

"*Black.*"

Steve nodded with a smile, threw in some coins from his pocket, and pushed a button on the machine.

A paper cup dropped. The machine hissed. The coffee started to pour.

Steve leaned against the wall.

"You really should go home," he said. "Get some rest. Take a shower. And please don't take this the wrong way, but you look like a bucket of baked assholes and don't smell much better either."

Mike didn't reply. Didn't smile.

Steve quickly realized that Mike was too fixated on one thing to think straight—and rightly so: Genevieve.

"We can't do much until we get that list, right? Check their list of known offenders in the area? That's our next step?"

Mike reluctantly nodded. Knowing they had hit so many dead ends.

Steve continued. "If the report isn't with me in the next couple of hours, I'll call the Bureau again, okay? I'll push them harder. And I'll let you know the *second* it comes in. I'll drive right over to your house and wake you up myself, okay? But you gotta go get some sleep."

Mike hesitated. He looked like he might argue. But

the fight left him for the morning. He nodded reluctantly, took the coffee, and walked out to his car.

———

The morning had soon turned to evening after Mike had returned home.

After a few hours of uneven and nightmare filled sleep, he was back in the living room, in front of paperwork piled on the coffee table. Photos, reports, old files. Of all past cases he kept copies of in his garage—not that it was allowed to copy any. He went through each file slowly, needing to make sure this was not linked to anything he had done before. Not thinking it was about him but wanting to make sure nonetheless so he could count that line of inquiry out. But the files that stared back at him told him nothing, mainly as he knew nothing. His daughter disappeared. That's it. No trace. No clues. Nothing.

The daylight outside had started to fade. The softest hint of orange from the still stormy evening sky bled in through the windows, just enough to keep Mike from needing to turn the lamp on to read.

From the kitchen, he could hear Toni talking on the phone. It was low, tired, worn down, just like he felt.

". . . The minute I hear anything, so will you," she said. "We'll talk later, okay? Bye-bye."

The receiver clicked into place, and a moment later, she appeared in the doorway to the living room.

"That was Tiana's mom," she said quietly. "She's a mess, just like me."

Mike stopped reading but did not look up, as he knew that something was about to follow. Some blame. Some jibe.

"She asked me why an official investigation hadn't been opened yet," Toni said with a shrug. "Like I'd know a thing. Like my own husband has kept me in the loop." She then stared bitterly. "*She* knows more than I do."

"You know I can't tell you everything that relates to—"

"An open investigation," she said, annoyed. "Yeah, yeah, I know the damn drill. You can't compromise the integrity of the investigation, blah, blah, blah. And you don't give a shit about the integrity of your wife, who's barely holding anything together."

Mike spoke emotionlessly. Not out of cruelty but out of needing to detach himself from the hurt he was feeling. "Toni, it's not going to help Gen if I let my worry as her father cloud my objectivity as a detective. I'm trying to find her."

"Well, it might help me if you told me anything." Her voice rose as she stepped closer. "Do you even hear yourself?"

He opened his mouth to speak, but she did not let him get a word in.

"Christ. For *fifteen* years, I've run second to your fucking job. Night shifts. Missed weekends. Cooking meals for your partners while you combed through bullshit files like this." She stared down at the cluttered table. "And how many times have I come downstairs to find one of them asleep on this couch? I treated them all like family, Mike. And the *one* time . . . *The one time* I ask for something, *really ask*, you give me the same line you'd give a stranger filing a report for a missing fucking cat." She was trembling. Her hands were clenched. "The department owes *me* after all I've done. I want you, Robbins, Steve, every one of you, to stop whatever else you're doing and find my little girl." Her voice cracked as the crying started. "Genevieve is missing, dammit."

Mike stood up from the couch and walked over to her, trying to hold himself together as best as he could but knowing he could not avoid this or brush it off. "You wanna know where we are?" he said, exasperated. "Huh? We are nowhere. We got nothing. Not a single fucking shred of any evidence. Does that make you feel better?"

As a reaction of sudden upset, her hand slapped him across the face. He didn't react, and she hit him again.

"*Please, Mike!*" she cried. "*It's been six days!*"

Mike didn't reply. He knew how she felt and didn't blame her at all. But admitting to her that they had nothing stung him just as hard.

She stood, waiting, breathing heavily, staring at him. Hoping he would say anything to calm her. Something he had kept back. Some confidential information that would blow the case wide open and bring her daughter home. But as she looked in his eyes, she could see that there was nothing.

"What are we going to do, Mike?" She wept quietly. "I . . . I . . ." She shook her head. "I don't know how long I can do this."

The doorbell rang, shocking her tears away. She stood there, staring at Mike, before turning and walking to the door. Hoping that Genevieve would be there as if on cue . . . and begged silently for it not to be a forlorn-looking cop carrying awful news.

She opened the door, dreading what would be waiting there.

It was neither her daughter nor a cop but her mother, Rose Stravelli. In her sixties, Rose was short, heavyset, carrying two heavy grocery bags in her arms. Beside her stood Angela, Toni's niece, a teenager just a little younger than Genevieve, who looked so much like her cousin that it hit Toni hard looking at her. The same long black hair. Same emo makeup. Same boots. It made Toni almost gasp.

Rose gave her a look. "So? You going to let us in?"

"What are you doing here?"

"I'm gonna cook you all dinner, 'cause I know for a fact you're in no fit state, and Angela is gonna do some chores."

Toni went to protest, but her mother just walked inside, not giving her a chance.

The kitchen was warm. Steam from a boiling pot had started to fog up the corners of the window above the sink. Toni moved around the counter, chopping quietly.

Rose sat at the table with a cigarette burning in one hand, dicing vegetables with the other.

". . . The warehouse prices are good, Mom, but who needs that much at once? What am I gonna do with a ten-kilo bag of potatoes?" Toni spoke softly, not really in the conversation. She was talking as if on autopilot. Her worry gnawed at her whole being and didn't give her a second's pause without thinking of her daughter.

"Well, it's good prices. You should come with me next time I go." Rose reached for the ashtray as she flicked her cigarette's ash into it. "Now how *are* you?"

"Awful," Toni said with a shake of her head. "I just wanna scream."

"You got every right to," Rose said as she lit another cigarette, not even finishing the first. "What about Michael?"

Toni didn't answer at first, just sneered. "The man of steel?" she grumbled sarcastically. "How do you think? We're both at each other's throats."

Rose shot her daughter a sudden glance of disapproval. "Hey, you know he's a good man," she said. "Last thing you both need is to be fighting. He must be torn apart, too."

"Him? Torn apart? Who can tell? He thinks nothing like me. Acts like nothing is going on. Show's no damn emotion."

Rose took a drag and stepped around the counter next to her. "When you were a little girl, do you remember what your favorite color was?"

"Yellow?" Toni smiled sadly. "Why?"

"*Everything* had to be yellow. Remember? Your room. Your bicycle. Your backpack. Your toys. You didn't want anything else. And your father and I, we let you have your way. We thought it was cute, so we didn't say a word. Hell, we encouraged it with all we bought you." She paused. "Maybe we shouldn't have. Maybe we should've insisted, once in a while, that you wore something else. Red? Green?" Her voice became more tender. "Because, baby, not everything in life *has* to be yellow. Not everyone is the same. Just because it's not yellow doesn't mean it's bad or wrong. Just different."

Toni understood her mother's clumsy attempt at advice clearly. She just couldn't fathom it. Of course Mike must have been hurting, too, but he should at least could've shown something to her. This was their daughter after all. Their only child.

Upstairs, Mike sat alone in Genevieve's bedroom, facing the monitor at her desk. The room hadn't been touched since she disappeared.

The same makeup lay scattered across the dresser. The same black hoodie was slung over her bed.

To Mike, it may have only been one hundred and fifty-one hours, but it felt like one hundred and fifty-one years.

He wanted to share his grief. He wanted to cry. He wanted to be there with Toni. But he had to be stronger. He could not let one chance to find her pass him by. He couldn't be her father right now.

He stared at the desk but didn't touch anything.

Walking by the open doorway, Angela, carrying a basket full of laundry, peered in.

"You online, Uncle Mike?" she asked.

"Uhh . . . What?" Mike only then realized that he was in front of the computer. His hands resting on the mouse and keyboard, he had not even noticed them.

Angela walked in and placed the laundry on Genevieve's bed.

"It's pretty cool," she said, motioning to the screen.

Mike turned to her in the chair. "It is? Why?"

"You can play games, message people. Hell, you can speak to people anywhere in the world. Talk in real time. It's more than just writing letters."

He shrugged. "Why not pick up the phone?"

"It's so much more. It's like a party, but everyone's invited." She smiled a little as she sat on the edge of the bed. "You see, I don't have to be me on there . . . Sometimes, I'm someone else. Like a prom queen or a cheerleader. Then I switch names and become someone totally different the next day. A wild girl. B-girl. Goth kid. Rich kid. Even an old man. I can be whatever."

She looked down, almost ashamed to admit.

"I've even met some people online. Cool people. It's a great way to make friends."

"You never met them in person, though, right? It's all on the internet?" Mike asked, realizing her sudden look of guilt. "Don't worry. I won't say anything."

Angela hesitated. "Well, yeah. A couple times, I have."

Mike felt his blood run cold. "Even Genevieve? Did she ever do that?"

Angela looked suddenly nervous. As if she was breaking a promise.

"Angela, please."

She reluctantly nodded. "Sometimes, sure. But everyone does it."

Mike's pager then went off. The beeping pulled him out of this moment. He checked the message but quickly switched it off. "Angela, you gotta show me how all this works, okay?"

In the kitchen, Rose was sitting at the counter, drinking a cup of coffee, as Toni was trying unsuccessfully to unscrew the cap on her beer bottle.

". . . Your father told them he doesn't care what the union did with that money," Rose said. "He's still expecting full benefits, or he's gonna rain down hell in court."

Toni, half-listening, twisted harder on the cap, and the bottle slipped from her hands, falling the floor and shattering in a mess of beer and broken shards.

This broke her.

She could not hold back.

She burst into total uncontrollable floods of tears. Crying harder than she had ever remembered crying before. The grief took absolute hold of her.

Rose was up from her chair in an instant. She

wrapped her arms around her daughter and held her tightly.

"Don't worry, baby," Rose whispered. "He'll find her. You'll see . . . Michael will find her. You gotta have faith!"

The door opened, and Mike walked in, too preoccupied to see the broken glass or the tears in his wife's eyes. He had his coat in one hand and car keys clenched tightly in the other.

"I gotta go out," he said, crossing to the hallway. "Back in a while."

Rose looked over to him as he walked away. "Has something happened?"

"It's nothing," he replied as he opened the door.

He was gone before anything more could be asked.

"See?" Toni said under her breath, staring at the doorway. "He doesn't care at all . . ."

———

The room was silent, with no natural light. Only the faint, candle flame placed on a metal tray by the far wall. A flame that barely held its own against the darkness.

The muscled figure moved. His bare feet pressed against the floor, carefully and slowly. His eyes had adjusted to the darkness, and he could see the shapes he passed behind. Unlit, unmoving, human-sized, yet no longer in spirit. They sat or hung or crouched, mostly indistinguishable in the dark. Bound and held captive.

As he walked close, one of the shapes stirred, just slightly as if it felt him nearby. A movement so small it might have gone unnoticed if not for how wrong it felt inside this stillness. A shuffle of life that caught the man's vicious attention.

He stopped in his tracks, watching the one that moved. Planning on what he could do to them next.

———

A mist drifted low over the tree and reed-filled lake. Moving in a thin sheet above the ground, clinging inches above all surfaces. The night sky was bleak. The storm clouds that still embraced Helvertown blotted out the stars and moon and only brought with it an uncomfortable chill. The only light here was the stutter of red-and-blue emergency lights by the lake's shoreline, which cast the cordoned off crime scene in a surreal light.

Mike's car approached slowly, headlights breaking through the mist as the scene took shape ahead. A crookedly parked news van sat off to the side, half on the grass near the stretch of yellow police tape.

He slowed near the cordon but didn't cross. Gravel crackled beneath his tires as he rolled to a stop and wound down his window.

From inside, he watched as two crew members argued with a pair of uniformed officers. One of the cameramen jabbed a finger toward the lake, voice raised, but it did not help. The officers stood firm.

They were calm and unmoved, and no one was getting past them.

One of the officers quickly spotted Mike and waved him through.

Driving on, he pulled out and drove past the cordon slowly, up to where the stone met the sunken reeds.

The lights from the cruisers flashed in shifting colors as Mike stepped out of the car and walked around to the trunk, popping it open.

Inside sat several boxes, each one labeled in bold black marker. Field kit. Evidence. Lights. Gloves. Masks. The tools of his job. Kept in a methodical and obsessive system.

He opened one of the boxes and pulled out two pairs of latex gloves. Snapping a pair on and pocketing the others, his eyes never left the dark lake ahead.

Since getting the page to call into the station as Angela started to tell him things about the internet he would rather not have known, his focus was spread thin. But he forced himself to be present here and not dwell on the million what-ifs that spiraled through his brain.

Several high-intensity flood lamps had been placed up around the perimeter. Their white beams bounced off the water in patches as officers moved around the shoreline slowly, talking in low voices, wondering what was down there. The hum of generators and police radios filled the rest of the air.

A few yards down the embankment, a tow truck sat parked with its back to the water. From a large winch, a steel cable trailed out and disappeared into the surface at an angle. Its hook deeply submerged into the lake.

At the back of the truck stood Detective Christian. His sleeves were rolled up, his expression frayed as he was speaking with a heavily tattooed truck operator.

Mike walked toward them, keeping his eyes on the lake, his boots crunching below.

The sound of his partners footsteps drew Steve's attention. He looked over, cut his conversation short, and walked over. He raised a hand to get Mike to stop. He didn't want his partner getting too close just yet.

"You sure you want to be here for this? You don't have to. I'd totally get it if you wanna go. Everyone would."

"I don't have a choice," Mike replied, scanning the illuminated water. "You know I don't."

With a nod, Steve led the way toward the lake's edge. The mist here was thicker and drifted up to waist height, making the discerning any details on the ground difficult.

Mike took a breath in. The smell of diesel from the generators, wet leaves, and mud made him feel sick. He was not a person who liked getting down with nature. He was a man who liked paved roads and central heating. Not someone who liked the elements. Especially now. *Especially* now. Everything here was uncomfortable and made so much worse with the reason they were here.

A few yards away, the two divers broke the water's surface, their heads rising slowly like ghosts in the floodlight's glare. One of them raised a gloved thumb. A signal that they had found what they were diving for and the hook was in place.

"You ready for this?" Steve asked gravely. "I can look first if you'd prefer?"

Mike avoided the offer. "Let's just get it done."

Matt Meyers, the tattooed truck operator, grabbed a metal lever and pulled down on it. As he did, the winch immediately shuddered into motion with a loud mechanical grinding noise. At the far end of the cable, as it was reeled back in, water began to churn as something heavy began to rise from the deep, pulled up inch by inch, as it broke free from the lake's bottom and rose to the surface.

Within a minute, the trunk of the car breached the water, coated in a thick sheen of grime and reeds that had been ripped up from the lakebed. From an older compact sedan, water poured out from every seam, gushing through cracks and taillight gaps in long, streams. A cracked bumper sticker clung to the back, barely legible through the clasped filth.

Mike leaned in close enough to read it.

Commit a senseless act of kindness.

"Fuck," he exhaled. "They were right . . . It's Tiana's car."

With Meyers controlling its descent, the vehicle soon hit the graveled ground with a dull thud and crunch of stone as its wheels dragged soggy reeds from the shore.

Officers moved closer, but Mike was already closer

and handed the second pair of gloves to Steve, knowing his partner would not be prepared. Which he wasn't.

"Nobody touches this vehicle," Mike ordered loudly. "Understand me?"

There was a chorus of muted affirmations as the uniformed officers and forensic examiners held back.

Steve walked next to him, putting on the offered gloves as his eyes scanned the exterior.

"How did the car get into this state so fast?" he asked as he picked off a string of weeds from the side.

Mike caught the movement. "Hold back until I say," he repeated.

"At the hip, remember?" Steve replied, without looking up, still looking at the car. "Captain's orders. We do this together."

Mike didn't argue. He didn't like it, but he remembered what Robbins said. He stepped to one side, letting Steve circle the front of the car.

"There must be a huge amount of this shit down there to cover the car," Steve said, looking over every part of the chassis that he could.

Taking his flashlight out, he swept the beam across the fogged and algae-slicked windows. The glass was clouded with a milky film, making it hard to determine what if anything was inside.

Mike hesitantly stepped forward as he braced himself. Grabbing the driver's side door handle, he pushed it down, and the lock clicked.

It creaked loudly as more water spilled out from

inside, sloshing over his boots, not that he noticed or cared.

Steve passed him the flashlight, which he took as he shined it inside.

Leaning in, he peered around. Over the seats, in the footwells, expecting to be confronted with the worst-case scenario . . .

. . . Nothing was there aside from a faint shape swaying from the rearview mirror. He brought the flashlight over it. It was an air freshener, bloated and stained from the lake water. Emblazoned with the phrase *MEAN PEOPLE SUCK* upon it.

Feeling some relief that it was so far empty, he moved back to the trunk, where Steve stood, looking worried for the worst-case scenario.

Steve knew that bodies were always put in the trunk if it was a murder in a ditched car. It was Murder 101.

The trunk soon popped, and a hiss of pressure escaped as the latch gave way. The heavy lid started to rise slowly.

Light soon filled the cavity as several heads leaned in beside Mike, officers, divers, and Steve.

They all stared in silence as they felt sick at what they saw.

The body inside was curled tightly, bloated from the water. Skin swollen and grayed, with matted hair. It faced away from them, small and still, floating just inches above the trunk floor in a pool of collected water.

Mike didn't want to. But he had to. Even. Though he knew who this was.

He reached in, steady and carefully, touching the shoulder and turned the body toward them.

The face came into view.

The vacant, dead-eyed stare of Tiana.

Her features were held in a horrified state. Eyes wide and mouth sewn shut. Thick, black thread looped crudely through her lips, pulling them closed with terrifying force. She had tried to scream. Mike could see that as the thread had ripped through her lips at a couple of points.

"Thank God," he whispered to himself. Mortified but relieved that she was alone in the trunk. His hope lessened but not yet dashed.

Camera flashes stuttered behind, followed by the low rumble of shouted questions as reporters breached the cordon. The instant they had realized that the police had found something, they rushed forward, barging the two officers out of the way.

Mike stepped back from the car, catching a breath as he tried to control his emotions.

Steve, meanwhile, leaned farther into the trunk, studying the inside with a narrowed gaze.

"Mike," he called out. "Look at this thing."

Mike turned, steeling himself and reluctantly looking back in. Steve's flashlight beam was locked on something metallic near the corner, wedged between flooded carpeting and the Tiana's bound heel.

Steve leaned in, reached down, and picked it out of the water.

Three inches long. Cylindrical. Tapered ends that

bent down into sharp points. Cold steel that was heavier than it looked.

"What the hell is that?" he asked, holding it up.

A voice answered from behind them.

"Looks like a septum spike to me."

They turned. The truck operator, Meyers, stood by the winch, watching them with interest. He was lanky and good-natured-looking, tattooed all down his arms and neck. A large bullring gleamed from his nose.

Mike stared back. "A *what* spike?"

Meyers pointed to his own nose as he walked closer. "Septum. But that one's thick as hell. Industrial gauge."

Steve held it out to him. "You sure?"

"Yeah, I'm sure," Meyers said, peering closer.

"What do you mean 'industrial gauge'?" Mike added.

"It's the biggest one I've seen," Meyers said, impressed. "A standard septum piercing is made with a fourteen-gauge needle. You can stretch it out to ten, maybe eight at a push. But this? This is a double-zero gauge. Get it? The owner of that spike has a hole in his septum big enough to fit your damn pinkie through. He must be real dedicated to the art."

Mike touched the bridge of his own nose, imagining the pain of forcing something like that through. "Dedicated?"

Meyers shrugged. "It's a monster. Anyone wearing that has a thing for pain. 'Cause that will hurt you even when the hole is healed."

Steve arched a brow. "You seem to know a lot for a guy hauling wrecks."

Meyers grinned. "Welcome to my world, Detective. You didn't think my only interest in life was ambulance chasing with this rig, did you?"

"What do you mean, your world?" Mike asked, quite confused by all this new information.

"Body art," Meyers replied. "Tattooing. Piercing. Branding. Scarification. It's about transformation. Self-expression. Been around since the dawn of man."

Steve snorted. "Yeah, right."

"We call ourselves modern primitives," Meyers said, unfazed. "We don't control the world. But we control this." He tapped his chest, then his face. "The body. And while everyone else is losing themselves to tech and virtual crap, we stay grounded. It's all done for tribal ritual. Heck, even Winston Churchill's mother had a tattoo. A small snake on her wrist."

That caught Mike's attention. "So, you are a *group*? In Helvertown?"

"More than you could know." Meyers smiled.

"Where do you all hang out?"

Meyers didn't hesitate. "Xibalba."

Steve squinted. "Zee-bal-ba?"

"It's a club in the city. In the old church on Belmont? You're gonna love it. But you gotta remember, despite what it looks like, we're all pacifists. This isn't about blood or pain. It's about identity."

Steve raised a brow. "What's does Xibalba mean?"

Meyers grinned again.

"The entrance to hell."

CHAPTER 4

THE ENTRANCE TO HELL

The drive from the lake was silent. The chill in the air seemed to have gotten colder the moment Tiana's dead, milky eyes stared up at them from the trunk of the waterlogged sedan. Mike sat behind the wheel, lost in thought, trying to piece together what they were about to walk into. He and Steve had taken Meyers' directions and decided to at least check it out. There was a reason that the septum spike was in the trunk, and this was as good a place as any to find out.

Neither of them had any idea that a club like the one Meyers described existed in Helvertown. Neither had even heard of it, let alone seen people who might frequent there. And the only reason that could be true was if the police never had to visit it on a case.

By the lakeside, Steve had called it in and checked the club's background. Sure enough, not a single police callout had ever been made. No raids. No fights. Even the local retirement homes had the occasional incident. But this place? Nothing.

That kind of clean record . . . was not usual.

But as they approached the address, Mike peered out of the windshield at the old church. One that he had seen plenty of times but never looked at. On top of it, a cross loomed, rusted and bold, bolted to the steeple of what was once a place of worship. Since then, its holy sanctity had been stripped away and gutted to a church of staining and mutilation, at least that's how Mike saw it. Below, where the faithful parishioners once gathered in wait for their sermon, stood a black-painted facade lit by a glowing red neon sign. *XIBALBA*, it said proudly.

Outside was a line of people pressed together in the cold night air. They wore leather, latex, chains, and studs as they waited to be let in. Many of them carried piercings of various sizes, across their faces, through the skin on their arms. Anywhere flesh could be seen. Tattoos wound down limbs and over heads, from geometric patterns, classic iconography, tribal swirls to name a few.

"They look miserable," Steve said, peering out the passenger-side window.

As Mike looked out, he saw it, too. No one here smiled. No one looked like they were having any fun. No one even seemed to blink as they waited.

That was true, especially the bouncers. The two men in suits guarded the entrance, wide and high like dressed up grizzly bears. Muscled Goliaths who would seem more at home in a war zone than outside filtering through patrons.

Mike pulled up in his car, rolling up on the curb, in front of a fire hydrant.

He killed the engine as he stared up at the imposing club.

Steve opened his door. "Let's get this over with," he grumbled as he stepped out.

He didn't wait for Mike to follow. He knew his partner would be right behind.

The bouncers squinted at the police badges they flashed. Neither cop nor bouncer spoke, but as the suited men stepped aside, they walked up to the entrance.

Mike gave the outside of the building a longer look. His eyes darted over the ornate arches, the old stone. He took a breath and stepped inside, knowing that what he was about to enter was not a world he had ever seen before.

The atmosphere changed in an instant. Outside was cold, emotionless, with the smell of asphalt and old car fumes. Inside, though, it was uncomfortably humid. A thick cloud of smoke covered the main dance floor as an electronic beat pulsed so loud that it hit Mike straight in the throat. That and the smell of flesh, sweat, and rubber, made him feel equally nauseous.

The strobing, spinning lights didn't reach every corner of the old nave, but they clung to what they could in ultraviolet, red, blue, and green pulses. And where the light didn't touch, in the booths that lined the back walls and the corners tabled around the side of large velvet clad pillars, people moved. Mike tried to focus on what these moving bodies were doing, but the shadows hid them all. All that *could* be seen was the undulating where rubber or flesh occasionally peeked out.

Shaking his head, he walked on. He didn't want to know. He was here for a singular purpose, to find the person who wore that septum spike. But as he looked at the multitude of gyrating pierced people, he realized that this would not be an easy prospect.

The music got louder the farther into the club they walked. It pounded at an extreme level that made even thinking straight difficult. It didn't invite you to dance. It more battered onto the floor and dared you to stay upright.

The congregation here was heaving. Bare skin and black clothing everywhere. Punks, bikers, goths, metalheads, any and all, now one as a mass of followers. People here moved with such lustful abandon that it shocked both detectives. They were all seemingly high or at least pretending to be. Each person looked lost in a rhythm that they had given themselves completely over to. Even the ones not dancing moved in time to the beat. In the nave, where once were pews, had been stripped, clearing space for the throbbing bodies. To Mike, it was like a scene straight from the pages of *Dante's Inferno*, where the damned all writhed in their own hell.

In the middle of the dancing throng, a statue stood

high on a revolving plinth. A black unicorn, rearing up. Its eyes had been painted all white, its horn shooting out like a large blade. Other painted black beasts rode beside it: a centaur with its hooves up high, a satyr in mid-scream. All of whom seemed deliberately grotesque, carefully constructed like some kind of holy icon to this crowd.

At the far end, where the altar once stood, was a stage where the music was being played. Guitars wailed through a maze of distortion and pedals as two drummers hammered the beat in a synchronized precision.

Only half of the dozen people on that stage were playing instruments. The rest were all performers. All in displays of pain or pleasure, flesh, or chains. They touched and cut and kissed in ways meant to be leered at. Sadism, masochism, with all bents of sexualities, on full display to everyone to see for the price of admission. Behind them, massive screens projected scenes that blurred the line between pornography and art.

Mike and Steve pushed their way through the smoke and sweat, feeling like strangers on a new planet. As they walked, the looks they got from the clientele ranged from amused to happy to lustful to almost hostile. These people didn't fear them. Didn't look at them worried like most other people in the town would. Usually, with police badges clipped to breast pockets as they were, it would elicit some sort of forced respect from the civilians. Even fake respect. Here, if anything, the crowds found them quaint and no threat.

Upstairs, the balcony had been marked by a sign that simply read, *NIRVANA*. Up the steps, it stank of sweat, cigarettes, semen, and cocaine. Across the tables and chairs, people lounged, pressed against the walls, wrapped around each other like wild animals in heat. Clothing was removed, and hands were everywhere. Mike didn't pause. Steve could not help but glance. But both kept moving. Meyers had told them the layout of the building, and they were following his direction across to the second main room.

Farther up, down another hall and through a double metal door, they found a large area lit only by a black light. Fluorescent paint covered each of the four walls. Images of patterns, symbols, erotic depictions, forbidden things, all looking as if a caveman daubed them. Some wore nothing except body paint that glowed under the light. Others were strapped into harnesses or suspended by ropes on large metallic frames. It was hard to tell who was conscious and who was acting in what seemed hardly legal to do in a public space.

The music here was no quieter than the main room. The speakers on the wall pumped through the same band at uncomfortable levels.

Mike looked around, at each person. He was lost. This club was disorientating and difficult for him to endure. He turned to Steve through the glowing light and gave a small shake of his head. It was obvious he felt some repulsion being here and wanted to go. "That's enough," he said, raising his voice over the music as best he could. "This is like trying to find the owner of the glass slipper in here . . ."

Steve didn't miss a beat. "Yeah . . . in a room full of Cinderellas."

"We won't be able to find anyone," Mike added.

"You wanna check the basement?" Steve asked.

"What's the point? Let's go back and make a plan."

Without another word, they turned around and made their way back toward the entrance. Back to their normality to work out their next move.

They did not enter the doorway on the other side of the room. The one that led to a beckoning spiral stairwell down into the sublevels under the church. A smaller sign at the top had been hand-painted in red over cracked wood. *Welcome To The Netherworld*, it proudly stated.

For those brave enough to walk down there, each step was darker than the last, until only the flame from a single candle guided their way. Even the music had faded to nothing down here. Replaced by an almost suffocating silence.

Passing through a narrow corridor lined with limestone, the candle at the bottom of the stairs threw shadows in wild dances along the walls.

Ahead was a door. Old, black, solid, and heavy.

Branded into its wood was a word that echoed the sign they'd already seen: *Netherworld*.

As the door creaked open, it revealed a vast stone

chamber. The glow of a roaring fire had been lit at the far end. The walls carried a dozen flaming torches around the room, giving the space a holy, ancient feel. The modern world felt a million miles away down here. Here where the smell of melting wax and burnt sage filled the air.

A woman, naked, shaved of hair from head to foot, sat with a drum between her legs. She beat on it in a slow, hypnotic rhythm. Her skin was covered in small, tattooed scales, and as the euphoria of this moment increased, her tongue, which had been split into a reptilian fork, licked her lips lustfully.

There, a small circle of people watched. Some knelt. Others swayed slowly to the drumming, heads bowed in reverence of what was happening in front of them.

From chains attached to the ceiling, suspended by hooks driven through the flesh of his chest, a man hung, motionless. Naked, muscular, and lean, he was covered in intricate tattoos from neck to toe. His arms hung slack at his sides, and his long dyed red hair draped down as he spun slowly in the air.

The watchers didn't seem alarmed.

A man with coral implants in his scalp that made him look like he had two horns broke the silence.

"That's it," he said. "Let him down."

Another voice came from the circle, quieter, less certain. "I don't think he's been up there long enough. He was really specific."

The first voice returned, sterner. "We don't want to *kill* him."

Silence again.

Then he repeated, "Let him down."

There was nothing at first.

Only darkness.

An absence of not just light of but of everything.

A total, absolute nothing.

Then, from somewhere, came a sound. A heartbeat, slow but growing louder. There was a faint buzzing that came with this pulse, like electricity flittering.

In this black void, from the middle of the nothingness, a single point of light soon came into view, hovering far ahead.

It didn't grow.

It didn't flicker.

It simply waited.

A voice came next, unmoored from a body. "Why am I not dead?"

There was no answer.

"*Why?*" he asked again.

"We had no choice. It was too much."

The heartbeat stopped. The buzzing fell away. The point of light vanished.

When his eyes opened slowly, his vision returned in fragments. The stone room around him was vague at first, with the surrounding figures shifting in and out of view. It took a minute for him to reorient as blurred faces hovered. As shapes moved in the firelight, each murmuring to one another.

"He told us to let him hang," said one.

"We're not murderers," replied another defensively.

The world soon settled into place as his haze cleared. He saw the horned man, leaning close to him, checking all was okay.

Without hesitation, a hand reached out and gripped the horned man by the throat. With tattooed fingers closing tightly, the horned man's breath was squeezed out.

The others in the circle moved back, startled but not interfering.

"I was almost *there*," the suspended man shouted, his voice rasping with exhaustion.

The horned man choked, tried to speak, tried to explain but could only wheeze.

Another voice came through the tension. "I thought you *were* dead."

The suspended man turned to them, then past them.

His fingers finally unclenched, and the horned man collapsed to the floor, coughing violently.

"The shamans call it the small death," the suspended man said, more to himself than to anyone in the room. "I was crossing it . . . I was crossing the abyss of life itself."

No one answered. They didn't know if he was speaking in metaphor or fact. He stood slowly, letting the pain settle through his limbs.

With one hand, he removed each hook from his chest, careful not to rip his skin.

"I was almost there," he repeated, baring his teeth. Each one, filed a point.

———————

Mike and Toni lay in their bed, neither of them sleeping, neither speaking. The tension between them didn't come from a fight. It came from what hung over each of them, what neither of them wanted to say aloud. Their daughter was not only missing but whatever, whoever, had her was murderous. There was no doubt she was in terrible danger now.

When the phone rang, it startled them both. Toni grabbed it immediately.

"Hello?"

Mike sat up. He watched her as she listened.

"Yeah. This is Toni Gage," she said, starting to look confused. "I don't understand . . . Who did you say you were?"

She didn't finish listening to the reply. Instead, she looked furious and slammed the receiver back onto its cradle with enough force to make Mike flinch.

"Who was that?" he asked.

Her anger was razor sharp. "Some goddamn fucking reporter," she grimaced. "He wanted to know if Gen was still alive . . . and if I thought that *you* were a suspect in all of it."

Mike reached out to her arm instinctively but

stopped himself short. He moved his hand back, quickly. Knowing she would not want him near her. She didn't notice. She just stared forward, into nothing.

Without a word, he got out of their bed and left the room.

The light from under the door crept out into the hallway. A toilet flushed, then Mike stepped out and padded back down to the bedroom, passing Genevieve's open door.

He stopped as he looked inside.

The room was dark as the rest of the house.

He hesitated before walking in and turned the lamp on by the bed. The soft light of the bulb filled the room with its calming light.

Everything was as it had been. He looked around, hoping to see something new. The makeup was on the dresser. A collection of perfume bottles. On the mirror on the wall, pictures were stuck along the edge. Photos of his daughter with her friends, including a strip from a photo booth of her with Tiana. They were both there, smiling happily. Mike moved closer and stared at the images, but the sadness started to get too much as the smiling image of Tiana changed into the image of her dead and bloated in the trunk.

He lowered his eyes to the shelf beside the bed.

A few stuffed animals sat there. A couple of old Barbie dolls. And a picture frame. It held a photo taken many years ago. He, Toni, and an eight-year-old

Genevieve sat on the beach. Sunlight. Sand. A happy, loving family.

Sitting on the bed, he sighed and picked up a small, stuffed duck that was on her pillow. Soft and worn. One of the toys from her early childhood. Once her favorite and still given pride of place. He stroked it gently.

He saw that her nightstand drawer was slightly open. Pulling it farther open, he peered inside. On top were several condoms, torn from their packaging, left on full display, casually. Mike's expression didn't change, but he felt the shift. Felt himself pull back into the role he knew he had to rely on. Detached, procedural. He left the drawer alone. She was no longer the child he saw in the family picture. She was a young woman. Sure, she was fifteen, but he could not think of her like that. She was Genevieve Gage, a missing woman. Not Gen, his daughter.

Shutting the drawer, he turned back to the desk. The computer sat there. He stared at it. He remembered what Ashley had told him. How she showed him the chatrooms.

He reached beneath the desk and plugged it back into the wall. Nothing happened. He waited. Still nothing.

He looked around, checked the screen, the keyboard, the tower. No button jumped out to be pressed. His hand moved over the casing, searching for anything to turn the machine on. But he found nothing.

Frustrated, he dropped back into the chair with a

heavy groan, staring at the computer in annoyance. He had no choice. He had to go against every fiber of his anti-tech being and learn to use this thing.

———

The morning had murkily arrived, with the gray clouds having returned to lord over the day, refusing to let and sunshine or warmth through.

Outside the police headquarters, officers lingered with their coffees, cigarettes and quiet conversations, having either just come on shift or about to knock off.

Mike climbed the steps from the car park, carrying two large boxes in his arms, one stacked awkwardly on top of the other. Fresh from the computer store, he had a brand-new laptop computer and had been talked into buying a computer to go with it.

He didn't speak to anyone as he passed. But they noticed him, grumpily walking inside.

Making his way through the busy lobby, he made his way back to his desk in the detective's bullpen. The surface of which was already cluttered with folders, notepads and coffee-stained memos, but he cleared enough space for his new equipment and dropped the boxes down with a resentful sigh.

The laptop was cutting edge—at least it was six months ago, and it now sat in front of him, powered up but still extremely unfamiliar. It cost him a month's salary, but he knew had no choice. He needed to adapt. For Genevieve.

Soon, he was thumbing through the pages of a thick how-to manual and read it without really taking any of the information in. It was all foreign in his eyes. Ram? Disk? Escape? Network? All words that meant something else entirely to him but meant something important to this machine.

Nothing felt intuitive with this machine. Not that he was the most susceptible student of any technology, but this was more difficult than most new things he had tried.

Beside the laptop lay something else, a copy of the glossy magazine *Tribal Age*, where, on the cover, the face of a woman stared out stoically. Her cheeks, scalp, nose, lips, eyebrows, were all marked by rings or studs, with decorative tattooing tracing up the edge of her jawline.

Putting the manual down, he grabbed the magazine, switching gears to try to understand something less complex. He started to turn the pages without much thought, scanning each photo in turn. They were stark, close-up, and unapologetically graphic. Bodies adorned, altered, transformed by piercings, ink, scarification, modification.

"Gage?"

He didn't hear Captain Robbins call out to him. He just stared at the pictures that seemed like alien pornography. As he stared at a picture of large breasts skewered by a steel needle, he realized that he somehow understood this culture less than he understood the laptop.

"Hey, Mike!" Captain Robbins said louder as he walked up beside his desk, holding a thin manila folder. "The coroner's report on Tiana Moore."

Mike reluctantly looked up from the magazine and slowly reached for the folder. Dreading its contents. Robbins held onto it, both holding onto it.

"They've confirmed she'd been dead for at least forty-eight hours before the car was pulled from the lake."

As Robbins let go, Mike took the folder and opened it.

The captain continued. "There's more."

Mike didn't want to hear more, as *more* was never good. But he nodded anyway. "Don't worry, Cap. I can handle it."

Robbins regarded him, then leaned down and turned the page in the folder.

"There," he said, pointing to a paragraph. "They found a series of puncture wounds . . ."

Mike saw it and read aloud from the page. "Symmetrically placed puncture wounds. Through the fascia and epithelial layers of skin. Face, breasts, and genitals."

He paused. Trying to take it in. He glanced down at the magazine.

"Damn . . . so it has to do with that piercing shit?" Steve sighed, having walked over, hearing just enough to react.

Mike shook his head and handed the folder back.

"The coroner says," Robbins said, "judging by the

crescent shape of the wounds, they were most probably made with a four-gauge needle. A surgical one."

Mike and Steve exchanged a look. Both remembering what Meyers had told them by the lakeside.

The captain continued. "None of the wounds, by themselves, were considered to be life-threatening. There was very little blood loss and no nerve damage."

"Then, how?" Steve asked.

"She had a heart attack," Mike sadly muttered.

"She had a congenital heart defect," Robbins confirmed. "It's likely the trauma she endured that brought it on."

Steve's tone shifted. "The puncture wounds did *that*?"

There was no need for Robbins to reply.

"She was tortured, and her heart gave out . . ." Mike said. His words didn't come with anger. They came with deep sadness. And a realization that the path they had been on was leading the right way, and that made the prospect of what his daughter was now going through that much more unbearable to fathom.

"You okay?" Robbins asked, looking down at Mike, worried.

"I'm fine," he replied through a grimace. "We need to continue the investigation systematically. We have the club. The septum spike. It's obvious now, with the report on Tiana, that we are dealing with someone who is into or knows about body modifications." Mike said, working it all out in his head. "That narrows the potential suspect pool down considerably."

———

Inside the colonial-style house, the room was just as it had been. The faint, candle flame was still placed on a tray by the far wall, throwing its weak light against the exposed brick walls.

The large shapes were still in the room, barely moving as before.

The man sat on a simple wooden stool, with his back to the shapes. On his lap lay a surgical tray, balanced across his knees. Each item on it had its place, neatly arranged. Hemostats. Forceps. Packs of sealed needles.

A sound slipped through the quiet. A restrained sob from behind him. A terrified sound.

The man's words came softly, not raised but clear enough to linger and drown out the whimper behind him.

"Where are the rites of passage?" he asked. "Do any of you know?"

He wasn't speaking to anyone in particular in the room, not directly. He was addressing something larger. The idea of something in his mind.

"Where are all the initiations for the young to endure? How can they ever hope to become true to their animal minds without the rites? Where are their struggles? The hardships? The tests of who they really are? Where is the pain to teach them what it is to live in the purest form of humanity?"

He picked up one of the sterile packages and peeled it open. Inside was an eight-gauge surgical needle, sharp and heavy, three inches long. He held it in his black-latex-gloved hand, turning it over between his fingers. He stared down at it in the faint candlelight, inspecting it as though he were admiring an ancient artifact passed down through generations.

"We live in a world filled with people wearing middle-aged skins," he mused. "Yet they stumble to a crawl with their childlike minds, filled with the basest of adolescent desires."

There was no hatred in his tone. Just observation. Disappointment. Confusion.

He touched the point of the needle to his forearm and pressed down, letting the tip push slowly through his skin.

"We must all go through our own rite of passage," he continued. His voice didn't waver from the new pain.

". . . And it *must* be a physical rite . . ."

His breath held in his throat as he pushed the needle in harder, sliding it through the top layers of flesh with a practiced control.

The needle went all the way through and out the opposite skin. As it did, blood began to gather along both sides of the entry point. He smiled at the warmth the pain had brought with it.

". . . It *must* be painful . . ."

He moved the needle gently, side to side,

encouraging the blood to flow thicker and freer out from the new wound.

". . . And it must leave an indelible mark."

His body tensed with the sensation as his breathing sounded closer to a pleasurable moan than a painful one.

He took hold of the metal tray with his free hand and stood up, the needle still lodged in his arm, the blood still dripping to the floor.

"What can we play with now?" he asked with glee. "More to the point, *who* can we play with now?"

Chapter 5

Entering The Modern Age

At the station, Mike sat at his desk, hunched over his new, confusing laptop. The printer had been set beside it, connected but otherwise untouched. He had worked through the instruction manual page by page, and as he did, his eyes strained and head ached. Every section on every page looked the same. Full of repeated technical jargon without any care if you didn't understand it. Even the glossary didn't help him get any deeper knowledge.

RAM: Random Access Memory.

What the hell did that explain?

He had spent the best part of the last hour just trying to connect to the internet. He had managed to power the laptop on and run through the initial setup guide that appeared on the screen. He had installed some software from a floppy disk that the screen had told him to do, not that Mike knew any of what was done or its purpose.

The internet login window for U.S.A. Online blinked, waiting.

Looking up from the book. Hoping he finally found the correct piece of information, he tapped out the keys slowly, carefully.

The cursor froze as he pressed the return key.

The box went blank again.

Incorrect user ID and password.

With a grunt, he reached for the manual again and flipped to the troubleshooting section, *again*, scanning for any answer.

He had asked Angela to show him some things, which she did, but he did retain a word of it.

He pressed a key on the keyboard.

He whispered a quiet plea. "Come on."

The screen blinked before going totally blank.

Mike slammed the manual shut and threw across the floor in frustration.

"*Motherfucker!*" he growled loudly.

Around the room, the other detectives looked over. No one offered help. They just stared before returning to their own tasks, pretending not to hear him.

Detective Steve was also sitting at his desk, but he did not turn away.

"Hey?" he called over quietly.

Mike didn't answer, too busy being annoyed.

Steve paused before asking the question anyway.

"How do you do it, man? How can you even see straight? I mean . . . She's not my daughter, and I . . ."

He didn't finish.

Mike didn't look over, but he had heard the question. "The only way I can help Gen is to put one foot in front of the other and do my job. Go through all this methodically. Without emotion."

He turned, meeting Steve's eyes with full intensity.

"I'm going to find her. Whatever way that turns out. I will . . ."

Steve broke the silence with a smile.

"As I am so damn tired of watching you try and dry hump your computer . . . Open 'Network Settings,'" he said.

Mike looked confused. "Open what now?"

Steve smiled and walked over. "What are you, eighty?" he quipped. "Here . . . Look . . ."

He leaned over and reached for the laptop's trackpad. With a few quick swipes, he navigated the menu as if it were second nature, which to Detective Steve Christian it was. When the first home computer came out, he was first in line to buy it. And with every new model, he upgraded every time.

"You click on the Internet heading here," he explained. "You see? And you click Wi-Fi . . . and there . . . See the police network? We just got it set up last year. One of the first in the whole country."

Mike nodded, seeing but not really understanding.

Steve stepped back, giving him control.

"Now move the cursor down to the Internet symbol . . ."

Mike looked lost.

"The globe one."

Mike held the mouse and followed the directions with careful attention, trying to remember everything. He was learning, not fast, but for him, even a baby step was akin to a giant leap.

The station was now quiet. Most of the desks were empty for the night, with the late shift officers either on patrol, or in the canteen, downing coffee. Only the low hum of the overhead light and the light ticking of a wall clock remained.

Mike was still at his desk, alone, eyes fixed on the computer screen in front of him.

Steve had gone through many other things about the laptop and told him how to get where he wanted. How to go online. How to save work. And Mike has written each lesson down step by step. Looking at the notes now, he felt proud of himself. He understood *some* of it, but more than that, he was online. He was in the chatrooms. The same ones that Angela showed him.

A chat window was open across the top of the screen. The heading stated: *Teen Chat Room 2*. His eyes scanned the details beaming out at him.

Names scrolled down the side, aliases from every

corner of the country—or at least that's what they said they were.

She had told him that a lot of people on here, were just kids messing around or old perverts looking for a thrill. But they were obvious to spot. So, here Mike was, with an assumed profile. A made-up name that Steve found hilarious when he set the account up.

```
SweeThang69
```

The other names on the screen confused him. He tried to read meaning into each one as he saw them. Tried to figure out why they were called that. What did their names show about them.

```
RitaJ22
CSend1107
Lovsik99
BlazJess711
Hardballin
Want2Peep
```

Mike had to pay attention to catch all the things that were being said as they buzzed by in the chat window. Most of it was meaningless. Random lines. Slang. Strange usernames cracking jokes or throwing questions into the digital void.

```
Where are you from, BlazJess711?
17/m
```

```
Je ne sais pas
Connecticut
What r the odds? Chicago being
such a small town and all.
Any female for phone talk here?
```

Many different conversations happened all over each other. It was dizzying.

But it was also time. Typing slowly with two fingers, Mike kept pausing every few letters, rereading his message. Making sure it was perfect.

```
SweeThang69: Hey, any of you dudes
wanna party harty?
```

There was a lull, a long pause.

Mike thought the connection had dropped. He checked the cables, made sure everything was still online.

One by one, the replies soon appeared.

```
BlazJess711: Party harty? What's
with that A-HOLE?
RitaJ22: Probably some pervert
lookin 4 jollies!
Lovsik99: Hey SweeThang69, HOW OLD
R U?
Want2peep: wow, faaar out!
Hahahahaha
KROQ1122: Classic rock lives,
```

Mike grimaced. The chat feed was exploding with a sudden vitriol against him. He didn't belong there, and the other users knew it immediately.

Embarrassed, he slammed the laptop closed.

———

A video camera sat on a tripod in the center of the candlelit room. Its red record light blinked, waiting to start. The large tattooed man with filed teeth adjusted the lens with deliberate care.

He looked through the viewfinder, adjusted the frame, and brought it into sharp focus.

In front of the camera, a naked teenage boy was chained to the wall. His mouth had been sewn shut with black thread, just like Genevieve and Tiana. It crisscrossed from lip to lip in tight stitches. He was awake, and his eyes were wide, filled with tearful fear, confusion and torment. His limbs had been forced into unnatural positions by metal bands locked tight across his arms, legs, and waist. They pressed into the flesh, reshaping it, holding him in place. Positioned just beyond the limit of how far they could bend but not too far, just enough so it caused the boy constant agony. Held at the pressure before any dislocation could occur. But that was not all had been done to him. Dozens of thin, stainless-steel needles pierced his skin in methodical patterns all over his body. From what he was enduring, it was only his terror of dying that kept him from passing out.

The camera beeped as it began to roll.

The tattooed man's voice came from just off frame soft and conversational as the image showed the full candlelit horror on display.

"The term 'sadism' is so maligned in our culture," he said. "If a doctor performs a hair transplant or a nose job, that's acceptable. That's okay. Applauded, even. But try and help another human being achieve a higher level of spiritual and sensual awareness by, oh, I don't know . . ." He paused as he savored the thought. "Piercing his genitals, and suddenly, *you're* the sick one. *You're* the monster. *You're* the evil."

The man stepped into frame, turned away from the camera. In one hand, he held up a large book, its pages open to a series of drawings. The images were all graphic, clinical illustrations of genital body modifications, each more extreme than the last.

"Which one do you want, then?" the man asked.

The boy shook his head weakly, unable to speak, unable to scream. He had little strength left, as his cries remained trapped behind the stitches.

Acting as if the boy had just pointed to one of pages, the man grinned as he turned the book around and looked at it.

"The ampallang, you say? Very well chosen," he said with a nod. "That's a master piercing. Few would ever have the nerve. I have one . . . Good on you."

His finger drifted over the drawing like it was his lover.

"Sure, it's a very touchy operation," he continued. "You've got to go through the spongiosum. And trust me when I say that it bleeds. *A lot*. And God forbid you hit the cavernosum, blood squirts all over the place like a fire hose."

The boy whimpered as his eyes begged for mercy.

The man didn't react.

"That said, there are tribes, like the Dayak in Borneo, where the women won't even consider having sex with a man who doesn't have one," he added. "And you should be glad—they use a long thorn to pierce, which can cause lots of problems. At least I have sterile needles."

More strangled cries rang out, but this time from other shadowed shapes in the room.

"So, what do you say?" the man asked rhetorically, ignoring the pained and weak chorus in the room.

The boy screamed as best he could through the sewn lips and depleted energy.

The man moved back behind the camera and zoomed in much closer, framing the shot, ready to capture what was about to happen in extremely close detail.

"All right, then," he said. "Let's have a whack at it, shall we? Let's make you a stud in the eyes of the Dayak!"

Turning to the surgical tray on the table, the man

grabbed a thick needle and took it out of its packet, then crouched on the floor in front of the boy.

Pausing, he regarded what he was about to pierce before grabbing a firm hold.

The needle soon found its place, and the smothered cries of the boy joined the terrified moans of the others watching this happen.

———

The storm had continued as Steve and Angela crossed the street toward the Police Headquarters. Angela was hunched beneath a newspaper, head down, shielding herself from the worst of it. Steve rushed beside her, not bothered about getting wet.

Mike had called him at home, waking him from his sleep, needing help, to which Steve had agreed without question. On the way, he had picked up Mike's niece, suffered her mother's complaints about the late hour but convinced her of the urgency nonetheless, something which Angela was more than happy to help with.

As the clock hit midnight, the bullpen was still mostly empty.

Mike and Angela were huddled around the open laptop. Online once more. Steve, meanwhile, leaned against a filing cabinet behind, watching silently as they searched through the chatrooms.

One room was open on the screen. A different one

to before, but now he was logged in under a new name. One that Angela suggested this time. One that was less suspicious.

```
RavesRUs
```

Angela watched as Mike typed out a line and hit Return key. The message appeared onto the screen instantly.

RavesRUs: Any "Bomb" fans here?

The messages quickly responded, not with any ire close to what Mike encountered earlier.

Msoftie321: Explosives?
ACoter7545: Yes!!!!!!
BJherel: Hey Msoftie . . .
nice head

Angela smiled as she pointed to **Msoftie321**.

"This one doesn't know who they are," she said. "Probably an old dude."

Mike glanced at her. "Is it a band?"

"Even *I* know that," Steve said from behind.

"I would have thought you meant explosives, too," Mike said with a smile. "Guess I'm old."

Angela rolled her eyes. "Type this . . . Tinsel, comma buttmunch, period. Tinsel Bomb, exclamation point."

Mike looked at her, confused.

"Type!" she prompted again.

"Okay, okay . . ." He began to type. "Tinsel?"

"Comma buttmunch."

Mike didn't ask, just followed direction.

She repeated. "Now, period. Tinsel Bomb, exclamation point."

Mike grinned and continued to type. "Which one's their name?"

Angela didn't answer. She just shook her head.

The chat feed lit up again.

```
ACoter7545: TINSEL BOMB RULES!!!!
BJherel: You go Raves!
Hard2hard: The Bomb are god!!!!
Cyco7983: Buttmunch? Asswipe!!
```

As they came in, Steve stepped closer and read over their shoulder. "Well, look at that . . . Detective Michael Gage . . . Computer wizard . . . I would have thought that was an oxymoron."

The phone on Steve's desk rang.

He walked over and picked it up.

"Detective Stephen Steve," he said.

He listened as he covered the receiver with his palm.

"It's the Internet guys," he said in a whisper.

Mike looked up and nodded. "Put em on speaker."

Steve placed the phone on his desk and hit a button.

"This is Detective Gage," Mike said.

"Uhhh, hi," a nasally voice replied through the

speaker. "This is Kyle Bendix, from U.S.A. Online. We spoke earlier?"

"Sure," Mike replied. "What d'you have for us, Mr. Bendix?"

"That list you asked for . . . I saw something—"

"Can you fax it through?" Steve interrupted.

Mike raised a hand to him. "What is it, Mr. Bendix?"

Bendix hesitated. "Well, there's one name in particular you might be interested in. The last person the user you gave, MissXXX, spoke to them before she signed off the chat room."

"Who?"

Bendix continued. "He or she used a stolen credit card and false personal info. Our system flags false payments up to fourteen days after an attempt and then we block the IP address of the user. Stopping them from getting online again. And this one was flagged earlier today. We don't have anything on them. Just the username. His IP also seems to be cloned."

Mike looked confused. "What's an IP?" he asked Angela.

She smiled and shook her head. "I can tell you later."

"Have you got a pen?" Bendix asked.

Mike grabbed his notebook.

"Uppercase C, lowercase A-P-T, uppercase H, lowercase O-W-D-Y."

Mike repeated it out loud. "CaptHowdy?"

"Captain Howdy?" Steve asked. "Like in *The Exorcist*?"

"I guess so," Bendix replied.

Mike looked at Steve, silently asking him to explain.

"The demon in *The Exorcist* calls itself Captain Howdy when the girl first meets it."

Angela had already grabbed the keyboard and started typing. Her fingers moved fast across the keys.

Bendix continued. "We haven't canceled this account as of yet, and I've put a hold on doing so until you tell us otherwise."

"Thank you very much, Mr. Bendix," Mike said.

"Have a nice night, Detective. I'll fax the list through now."

Steve hung up the call.

"So, *The Exorcist*?" Mike asked. "You think we got a devil worshipper on our hands?"

Angela looked up. "He's here."

Mike turned. "Who?"

"Captain Howdy," she replied casually. "I used the 'Locate a Member Online' function."

Steve smiled. "Awesome."

Angela pointed at the screen. "People use it all the time. It's in the pull-down menu. Helps us see more about the names. Not much, but it's something... There you go."

The screen showed the result.

```
CaptHowdy is in Teen Chat 7 in
People Connection
```

Mike took over the mouse and clicked through the menus with more confidence. Remembering the navigation from the *departments* list, through to the sub-menus. He clicked, one window leading to another. Finally, a list of public chat rooms appeared in a box. His cursor scrolled down the column until it stopped at one: Teen Chat 7.

The room opened.

They were in.

RavesRUs: you have joined Teen Chat 7

In the Colonial-style house, the man with filed teeth, the man calling himself Captain Howdy, stared at a computer screen.

Somewhere outside, a dog barked without pause, distant but constant.

On the monitor, a new name had entered the chat room. It appeared at the top of the user list.

RavesRUs

He watched the name for a moment, moved his mouse, clicked on it, and opened the user profile.

Birthdate: 12-7-78

```
Hobbies: Dancing, water skiing,
industrial music
```

He stared at the screen as he let out a soft groan of approval.

Mike sat closer to the laptop, his attention fully fixed on the chat room, with Angela still beside him, Steve behind, all watching the same screen.

In the chat room, names were listed down the side as conversations scrolled up the main feed.

Mike had clicked on the *People* icon and opened the list of active users.

There was *that* name; `CaptHowdy`.

"Okay, he's there," Steve said. "Now, how do we draw him out?"

Angela didn't hesitate. "I know what to do. Open up his profile."

Mike clicked on the name. A new window opened, filled with Captain Howdy's profile, an assortment of convincingly fake personal details.

Angela scanned the information. "No wonder people like him. This looks like a very cool guy."

Steve looked at the same details. "How do we even know it's a guy?"

Angela shrugged. "We don't—that's part of the fun."

The cursor hovered over the hobbies line.

```
Hobbies: Street hockey,
snowboarding, going to concerts
```

She pointed at the screen. "Quick, open up your profile. Highlight the hobbies section and delete 'water skiing.'"

Mike followed the instructions.

"Now put in . . . uhhh . . . 'winter sports.'"

Mike made the edit and nodded.

He looked at his niece and raised an eyebrow. "Have you considered a career in law enforcement?"

Captain Howdy narrowed his eyes at the screen.

The profile information for RavesRUs had just changed.

He saw it happen in real time.

He chuckled quietly to himself.

"There are thousands hacking at the branches of evil," he muttered quietly, "to *one* who is striking at its roots."

Mike closed out his profile window and returned to the chat room. Howdy's name was still there.

Angela didn't hesitate. "Ask if there are any snowboarders in the house."

Mike typed the question and sent it. The conversation on the screen continued to unfold, scrolling line by line.

A new message appeared.

CaptHowdy: Hey Raves, what kind of
boarding do you do?

"Tell him half-pipe freestyle," she said. "Then ask
what kind of board he uses."

Mike typed it out and hit *Return*.

There was a pause.

Then the response came.

CaptHowdy: I trashed my old board!
Just picked up a new Burton.

A chime sounded. A new window popped open on
the screen.

An instant message, sent directly to RavesRUs.

CaptHowdy: Hey Raves, you want to
come to a party?

Mike leaned back in his chair, eyes on the screen,
feeling a sense of victory.

"Gotcha," he grinned.

Angela looked at him, hopeful. "So, how'd I do? I
helped, right? We'll find Gen?"

———

The rain had followed them across town and into this more affluent neighborhood.

The street was quiet as the clock hit 1 a.m. and was illuminated with subdued street lighting. The houses here were wide-set, well-kept, lined with trimmed hedges and closed blinds. Driveways were filled with newer, sensible cars. It was the kind of place that eschewed safety and privilege.

That illusion faded quickly as the police arrived.

From the vans and cruisers that had quietly approached and parked in formation, tactical police units quickly stepped out. Men in black body armor and helmets, carrying semi-automatic rifles, fanned across the lawn of one of the colonial-style houses. They flanked the building from all sides as they took cover behind hedges, crouched beside parked cars, and posted themselves at each corner. The operation was clean, practiced, and most of all, silent.

At the front door, one of the officers took position with a battering ram. Behind him stood Mike, Steve, and Robbins. All three were focused, their handguns drawn. Their badges on chains around their neck rested over thick bulletproof vests.

A voice shouted out. The commander of this SWAT team.

"*Police! We have your house surrounded.*"

The ram hit the door with a crack like a cannon. The lock shattered on impact as the wood split, giving way.

The team surged forward through the broken doorway.

Inside, the house was full of shadows as police flashlights swept through hallways as boots hit on tile and wood.

They progressed at speed throughout the house.

Every door was kicked open.

Each room was cleared with weapons raised and orders called out.

They advanced to the second floor.

Mike quickly moved to the front of the procession of armed officers, his flashlight shining through the darkness of the house.

They soon came to a closed door at the far end.

"Police!" Mike called out. "Show yourself with your hands raised!"

He quickly barged through the door. Flashlight beams flooded the room.

In a state of terror, two figures froze. An elderly couple, both tangled in blankets, both in a state of shock. The man had trouble catching his breath. He began to move, reaching toward the nightstand.

In that instant, every weapon in the room turned on him.

"My pills," he cried out in desperation.

And there, on the nightstand, sat a small medicine vial.

. . .

Outside, in the rain, Robbins stepped out of the house, onto the covered porch, sliding his gun back into its holster. He walked over to Steve, who was standing on the front step, smoking a cigarette.

"That went well," Robbins said dryly. "Where's Gage?"

Steve motioned across the street.

Mike was in his car, parked under the shadow of a maple tree. His face was barely visible through the streaked windshield.

"Can't imagine what he's going through," Steve said.

Robbins didn't look over. "Hell."

Inside the car, Mike sat without moving. The engine was off. The windshield wipers hadn't been turned on. He stared out, but he wasn't watching anything.

His thoughts weren't on the failed raid but just on his missing daughter. That he was somehow letting her down. That a mistake like this could have a high price.

Steve appeared at the passenger-side window. He tapped the glass.

"You want company?" he asked.

Mike shook his head.

Steve didn't press. "Well," he said, stepping back, "try and get some sleep, okay? See you tomorrow." He hesitated. "We'll get this fucker. You can be damn sure of that."

As his partner walked away to get a lift with another officer, Mike started the engine. Reaching up to adjust the side-view mirror, he paused as he caught his own reflection.

The face looking back at him was exhausted and a shell of who he usually was. He stared for a while before shutting off the engine again.

He didn't know what to do.

What would going home give him? More arguments. More blame from his wife that this was his fault. Sleep in a house that was filled with reminders of Gen?

He reached for the files on the back seat and began to pull them out, spreading them across the passenger side. Case reports. Photos. Chat transcripts. Names. Dates.

He wasn't going to go home tonight. This was as good as office as any. At least he brought his laptop.

The closet was small, barely big enough for one person, and even with the light from the hallway, it somehow felt smaller. Toni Gage was peering in. Standing pressed against the hanging coats.

Her fingers reached up, blindly searching the top shelf.

The shoebox she needed had been pushed to the back, and she had to stand on her tiptoes to even stand a chance of reaching it. When she finally managed to grab one corner and pull, she nearly dropped it in her relief.

She fumbled with the lid and looked inside.

There lay a small bag of weed. Rolling papers. A few ready-made joints in a sealed container. A half-empty pack of matches.

This was her emergency box. One she hadn't needed to look in for a very long time.

She didn't think. She didn't pause. She took one of the joints out, sank to the floor in the hallway, and lit one with a match held in a shaking hand. The first drag she inhaled was too deep, held too long and exhaled hard through her nose. Immediately pulling her into a daze.

Her eyes flicked around the hallway, making sure no one was watching her, even though she knew full well that she was alone in this large house. Even so, if Mike had been home, she would still have done this? Yes, she would.

The smoke settled around her shoulders like a blanket she desperately needed.

CHAPTER 6

LET ME AWAKEN YOU

The morning was breaking on Harrow Street outside a row of colonial-style houses. The chaos of the police raid the night before had long since passed. The storm had swept through, wiping the slate clean, and it had left everything rinsed. The sky had started to pale, but the sun hadn't yet made its full appearance.

From a nearby house, a door to a backyard opened and a dog burst out onto a patchy lawn, and within seconds, its barking shattered what was a calm stillness. Loud. Urgent. It barked at the trees, barked at the sky, barked at the air. Barked at anything and nothing. Warding off any dangers the dog felt it needed to.

Mike jolted awake in the front seat of his car. Woken by this sudden noise.

He wasn't sure when he'd drifted off, but it wasn't that long ago. He had reread all the files he had at least five times over. Hoping to find something he had overlooked. A small detail that would prove to be the key to the case.

Wiping the sleep from his eyes with his palm, he shifted upright in his seat and grabbed his laptop from the footwell beside him.

He picked up the cell phone, tapped through a few commands, and dialed into the internet. On the laptop, the connection clicked and whined through the speakers, the familiar sound like a scream from inside the machine. When it cleared, the screen filled with light and words.

`Welcome to U.S.A. Online.`

Forty-eight hours ago, he would have balked at not only owning a laptop but having the know-how of how to go online through his cell phone of all things.

The chatroom webpage opened up where he left off.

He logged in.

He navigated through the system to open the member directory—

A chime rang out of the speakers as the messenger loaded. The sender had been waiting for his name to flash online.

CaptHowdy: `Where have you been, Raves? I've been waiting all night. Or should I call you 'cop'?`

As Mike read the words, a chill fell over him as he

realized that this was a game to Howdy. They knew they had been set up and been given a fake address, but now Mike knew something else, Howdy had seen them. Knew what was happening.

He typed a reply.

RavesRUs: Call me Detective. Tell me who you are? Some sicko?

The screen paused, cursor blinking at him as he waited for a reply.

Another chime.

This one wasn't text.

A new window opened with controls: rewind, fast forward, play, record. A video had been sent to him. He clicked play.

The voice came through the speakers. Playing its recorded message.

"Tsk, tsk. Using the concept of 'sicko' to minimize and disparage draws a veil across a reality you are in no position to interpret. Nice show last night, though. I hope you weren't too disappointed? They are such a nice couple."

Mike looked around the screen and saw the red button that said Record beneath it. He instantly clicked on it, hoping it would work, though not knowing for sure.

"It's all part of the job," he replied clearly, trying to sound as calm as possible. "It's all part of finding you."

He pushed all thoughts of his daughter as far down as he could, staying cold and emotionless.

He clicked on the stop button, and the recording was instantly sent through the ether.

Another pause. Another chime. Another recording came through.

"Ah, there's nothing like a heapin' helpin' of testosterone-ladened, false confidence, is there?"

Outside the car, the dog was still barking. Too loud for Mike to hear properly. He paused the recording until the animal stopped its tirade, then pressed play again.

"And there certainly was a lot of that at the big bust, wasn't there? It was a real swinging of dicks and guns. So exciting . . ."

But something was different in the recording. Mike heard something else. He hit play on that message again. Playing it back from the beginning.

There was dog barking. *That* dog. Not outside. On the message he was listening to, there, in the background of Howdy's mocking. Close. He played the message once more. It was unmistakable. Soon, the real dog outside barked again, and from the playback, the second bark layered into it.

The first real clue of where this suspect was.

He moved the laptop onto the passenger seat, on top of all the files, leaving the chat window open.

The key turned in the ignition. The engine choked to life, and Mike pulled out slowly. The windows wound down. He let the sound guide him like a compass. The dog barked louder the farther down the block he went.

With one hand, he turned to the laptop and clicked the record button.

"You're an intelligent man, I presume," Mike said loudly. "Why don't you give yourself up? You know it's only a matter of time, right?"

Outside, the barking hit a pitch that sounded as close to him as it was to Howdy.

He rounded a corner, and there the animal was. A plain house on a plain street, same as every other in this neighborhood. The dog barked from behind a wooden fence, hackles raised.

Mike pulled to the curb, parked and stared.

The door to the house soon opened.

A man stepped out in slippers and a loosely tied robe, balding, his eyes squinting against the morning brightness. He picked up a bagged newspaper from the porch steps, glanced once at Mike's car, and froze. Self-conscious, he could see Mike looking back at him. Quickly, he adjusted his robe and turned back inside, the door closing behind him.

A chime. Another message from Howdy.

The same voice came through the speaker.

"Really, Detective. Don't you find a victory by forfeit to be a hollow one? Come on . . . find me. It's a hunt. A primal hunt like the starving settlers on the plains looking for food in the barren wastes. Really dig deep to live another day."

Mike didn't need that encouragement.

He closed the laptop, stepped out of the car, and walked toward the barking.

The dog's yard ahead lay next to another house. One that immediately made him stop in his tracks. At first, it looked normal but the more he stared the stranger it looked.

The outside of the colonial-style house was perfect. White picket fence. Perfectly manicured lawn. But as he stared, he saw there we no curtains. No shutters. Not a decoration, not a sign of life. Every single pane had been blacked out. Not shaded but painted on the inside of the glass. Not something any usual house would have. He knew that if the windows were blacked out, whoever was inside could most likely not see out either.

He had no patience to wait for backup as he hurriedly moved to the porch and drew the revolver from his shoulder holster.

Getting to the front door, he stared at the bell, weighing his options.

Better to be let in, he thought.

He rang the bell with the butt of the gun and waited.

But no sound came from inside. No bell sound. No footsteps. No calling out to hold on.

He rang it again.

Still, no ring could be heard.

He changed gears and knocked, heavy and loud.

"Hello? Is anybody home?" he shouted.

No answer.

Mike moved off the porch and over to the nearest

window. He tried to peer through, but all he saw was the paint, applied thickly from the inside. There was no way of seeing in. He then moved quickly around the house, checking each window in turn. Hoping one would be clear, but they were all blacked out in the same way. Hiding something within.

Around the back, this pattern continued. Painted glass on the windows and doors. Ahead sat a small garage, with a pair of heavy iron cellar doors sunken into the grass beneath it. Old-fashioned, like something meant for coal deliveries, not modern life.

Mike crept over, tiptoeing carefully across the gravel. Keeping an eye on the house next to him at all times, he could see that the top half of the garage's sectioned windows were narrow but clear. No paint.

He had to stand on his tiptoes to look inside.

Sitting in the shadow was an old Lincoln Continental, in perfect yet dusty condition. The shelves around it that lined the garage walls carried the usual items: boxes, tools, yard gear. Nothing remarkable. Nothing suspicious.

Waking on, Mike came to a row of open garbage cans on the opposite side to the garage door. He stopped and tore one of the top trash bags open.

Inside was just ordinary waste. Soda cans. Food cartons.

He moved to the next one can and did the same.

But this did not have trash inside.

Among the cladding of bloody tissues, something glistened out at him.

He leaned closer to see.

Two surgical needles lay wedged between the red-stained fabric. Reflecting the morning light like the edge of a blade.

He reached down, grabbed a clean, unbloodied corner of the wadded tissue and pulled at it. As he did, dozens of needles spilled into view. Different needle sizes.

His heart picked up pace. *This was it. This was the man. It had to be.*

He had to get in.

Turning toward the iron cellar doors at the base of the house, he noticed that a heavy lock hung from the latch. Appearing large and solid, it was still years past its prime. Rust had claimed most of its body, making the metal much weaker. More breakable.

He turned his sight around the overgrown yard. Near a strip of wire fencing, half-buried in the weeds, he could see a brick, weathered but intact. Perfect for what he needed.

He picked it up with his free hand, weighed it with a hopeful smile, and returned to the cellar doors.

With a breath drawn and his gun temporarily holstered, he brought the brick down hard on the lock. Once. Twice. The sound was loud and jarring. On the third blow, the rusted metal gave way with a brittle snap.

He knew that Howdy must have heard this, but maybe he passed it off as a neighbor working in his yard. Or maybe he was there, waiting for him to enter. Either way, Mike had no choice.

He let the brick fall to the grass as, with both hands, he grasped the handles of the cellar doors and pulled up. They resisted at first, their hinges stiff. But slowly, they soon opened, revealing an abyss of darkness below a set of concrete steps, exhaling a waft of cold, moldy air.

The morning glow filtered in from behind him just enough to make out the dirt floor below.

He drew his revolver again and descended one stair at a time. He knew he should have called for backup. But it was too late now, and nothing could stop him. Certainly, there was no way he could wait by his car for others to arrive.

The smell of vinegary, sour sweat hit him before he reached the dirt floor. He reached into his coat and pulled out a pocket flashlight. Flicking it on, he saw the beam quickly reveal a collection of handmade gym equipment down here, all fixed together from scrap steel and bolted to the concrete floor. Across from them, a long workbench stood to one side. One that was cluttered with tools.

His light passed over a welding mask. A mannequin torso. A metal bar. A coil of metal wire. A hot water heater, washer, dryer, and a small furnace. And lying between them, a narrow staircase led up to the house.

Moving on with steady, very measured steps, he checked behind each object in the room as he walked toward the staircase. Gun leading his way, ready for any surprise that may be waiting.

Mike was already at the top of the steps before he noticed. Crouched low, slowly easing the door to the house open.

It creaked low and soon exposed the darkness on the other side.

Switching his flashlight off, he kept it in his hand, ready to turn on at any moment. He stepped through as quietly as possible. Howdy may have heard him break in, but he would not hear where he was in the house.

The only light he could see came only from the flickering flames of candles set at uneven intervals along the hallway in front of him.

Letting his eyes adjust to the low light, Mike stepped soundlessly on hard floor and moved on.

Entering a reception room, he peered up at the staircase to the next floor, then to his and his right and left, where sets of sliding doors were closed.

As he waited, he began to smell something. A terrible rising stench of human excretion. Following the smell up to one of the closed doors, he placed his ear closer to the wood. There was no sound.

Against everything in his body screaming at him to leave, Mike put one hand on the door and slid it open.

The smell was more pungent inside and hit him as soon as the door opened. So much so, he had to fight against the urge to retch.

This was, at his best guess, a living room. He could see the original shape of the structure as he looked through the gloom. A collection of ineffectual candles lit were by the door, weakly trying to brighten up the few feet around them, but they exposed little.

Turning to one side, he could see that wall had been covered from floor to ceiling in thick acoustic foam. Foam that absorbed sound, masking noise from being heard outside.

A scrape.

Sudden.

Low.

Ahead.

Alerting Mike in an instant. He had no choice but to turn on his flashlight.

The beam cut through the black and landed on the far side of the room. At first, it looked like a collection of thick shadows, but as he stared, that darkness started to move. Very quickly, his eyes could see what was in front of him. Young men and women, barely out of their teens, some not even that. They had been stripped naked and were hanging limp on various thick metal restraints. Tethered, bound, and suspended onto various benches and racks, contorted into uncomfortable and painful shapes. Legs chained too far apart, heads strapped as far back as they could go without breaking a bone. Each one of the devices they were upon were homemade and welded together like the workout bench downstairs.

These weren't just prisoners. They were being held in states of torture. They had obviously been here for a while. Catheters ran from their groins, collecting the urine into bedpans, but nothing had been done about the feces. Their bodies were stained with their own waste, a *lot* of their own waste, fallen over themselves multiple times over multiple days.

Mike could not move as he stared in abject horror. Not able to fathom the sight of torment.

These kids were not only tied up but were each in some different state of violation. Some had limbs contorted by leather straps and razor wire; others were pierced, laced, sewn, or split. Each of their mouths had been sealed shut like Tiana's. Some sewn with black thread, others wired closed with lengths of metal.

And as Mike stepped closer, each tried to move, alerted to his presence. Those with enough strength to open their eyes immediately realized that this was not the man who had hurt them. Even half-conscious, their instincts fought to reach out to him. Any arms that were not bound raised, trembling. Arms. Legs twitched. Heads lifted as much as they could, and the moans came next. Muffled, muted, and very desperate. A chorus of panic, pleading and agony.

His hands trembled, blood ran cold, and he felt a rising of sick and panic. Turning his flashlight, the beam hit on the far wall, where a teenage boy hung chained from the ceiling by both wrists. His body bore the pattern of long, deliberate lashes, crusted over with blood and open welts. His penis had been skewered multiple times with long, thick metal bars. Next to him, another girl stood motionless, tied to a metal stake, forced on her feet. Her entire body had been wrapped in gold leaf. Her skin shimmered in the light like a statue. But she was alive. Her chest rose and fell slowly beneath a mask that covered her entire head, sealed with a deprivation helmet, designed to blind, silence, and suffocate the senses. Only a thin breathing tube gave her access to air.

There was another next to her. A small cage, too small, where a girl was crammed painfully inside, curled in on herself, filling up almost every inch. Her body was covered from head to foot in tiny piercings. Small rings broke her skin from neck to breast to groin to feet. She was shaking, her face contorted in silent shock.

Next to her, a boy had been stretched out in a parody of crucifixion. Nailed upside down to a wooden cross, his limbs were swollen from hours, maybe days of suspension. His mouth was sewn like the others as a steady stream of saliva, and blood ran down his face. His eyes blinked with staggering slowness.

Then came the bed of blades. A man lay face down across it, bound at the wrists and ankles. The metal tips were carefully arranged to support just enough of his weight to prevent fatal impalement but not enough to stop the blood. It ran in quiet drops down to the floor, soaking into the floorboards beneath.

And finally, among the many sights of torture, his beam found her.

Genevieve.

Her body was wrapped in lines of fishing wire, crisscrossing around her limbs and torso, cinched so tightly that the flesh bulged out between. Her skin had been punctured again and again with long, silver piercing needles that glinted in the flashlight's beam. Blood had dried around these punctures and were dark red and starting to look infected.

Her face was incredibly swollen and bruised, but her eyes were open. Staring up at him in tears. Tears that had not stopped since she had entered this house with Tiana.

Mike rushed over to her, passing all the other tortured bodies, holstering his gun as he started to cry, too, but with rage mixed with relief. His hands were already searching for a way to pull the wire off her, to pull the needles out, to save her. But his whole body was shaking. His fingers found it difficult to find the way to release her.

Genevieve's eyes were opened even wider as she saw something over his shoulder. Something horrifying.

She thrashed, moaning, her head jerking violently to one side, trying anything to get her father to stop, to see that something was coming from behind him, fast, through the doorway.

Mike realized the warning too late.

He half turned, confused, just as the blow came down upon him.

A heavy impact came from the side, knocking him clean off his feet. He landed hard against a wall, his gun knocking out of his holster and skidding across the floor.

The lights in the room then switched on. Not a usual bulb but a brightly colored, bloodred one. Which soaked the whole room in an almost blinding crimson hue.

Mike rolled onto his back, stunned, and saw what had collided with him, in all of its detail.

Captain Howdy.

He was huge.

Naked.

Furious.

His body was split down the middle with ink. One half was a canvas of dense, jet-black tribal tattoos, curling and clawing up his ribs, over his chest, across his neck and face. Even half of his lips had been darkened into a permanent black sneer.

The other half was pierced. Completely. Bars, studs, hoops, wires. From the crown of his head to the sole of his foot, this side of his body looked like it had been dragged through steel.

His hair was half shorn. The tattooed side was long, dyed a neon red, while the pierced side was shaved totally bald.

In his mouth, which growled at the detective, his teeth, every last one, had been filed to a point.

He came in like a fury.

Mike scrambled, lunging toward his gun, which lay a few feet away.

He managed to grab it just as Howdy raised his fist.

Before the pierced Goliath could land another hit, the gun was aimed and fired.

The first shot hit Howdy's thigh.

He screamed but not in pain.

In a rage.

A consummate anger that someone else aside from him had the upper hand. Had gained any control.

He dropped to one knee as the injured leg gave way.

Mike didn't wait. He climbed to his feet and charged, aiming the barrel of the pistol hard against Howdy's skull.

"On your stomach," he barked. "Hands behind your head!"

Then, in a sudden switch, Howdy stopped any resistance. His angry grimace fell in an instant. Turned off. What was left was a small smile as he slowly lay on the floor, breathing hard. Bleeding. But eerily content.

He showed zero restraint as Mike roughly cuffed him.

He just lay there with an unnervingly compliance. So much so that Mike peered up at the doorway, expecting it to be a trap. That he was playing possum to keep him busy while something else came at him.

But nothing did. Howdy had just immediately given up as if it were a game.

With the man cuffed and on the floor, Mike rushed back to his daughter.

"It's okay," he said, pulling the wires away from her skin. "You're all right. I'm here." His voice cracked as the emotion came flooding back. "Everything's gonna be all right. I'm here. I'm here . . ."

Behind him, Howdy shifted in place and sat upright, still smiling with his hands locked behind his back. As he spoke, he stared at the ceiling like it was a window to his heavens. "You see," he said. "I've never been afraid of anything in my whole life . . . Do you want to know why?"

Mike turned, his eyes locked on the man. He said nothing.

"Do you want to know *why?*" he asked again, more pointedly.

Howdy smiled as he kept looking upward. "Because I wish I were dead." His gaze fell to Mike's. "And when you wish that, there's nothing left to fear. I have only pain to live for. It's my only pleasure." He leaned slightly forward. "But even hatred runs dry . . . I fought. You shot me. You bound me. You beat me in this moment. I accept that. I don't care. I am now here for the silence to come." He angled his head with a curious expression. "What do you see here?"

Mike still did not reply.

"I bet you see abuse . . . Torture . . . But it's not pain I gave them. It was clarity. You see the difference, don't you? They only screamed because they were waking up. I was just the alarm clock. And now . . . Now it's my turn to wake up from this life . . . So, Detective, pull the trigger. Just do it . . . Exact whatever rage you have on me. Kill me. Let my final pain pleasure you. Let me awaken you."

Mike stood up from Genevieve, pulled a napkin out of his pocket, walked over, and shoved it into Howdy's mouth.

"I do wish you were dead," he said. "But I won't do you that favor."

. . .

An hour later, the room looked very different. It was brighter. The candles were gone. The windows had been broken open to let the daylight in. Flashbulbs popped. Paramedics and forensic examiners moved through the whole building carefully, removing the last of the survivors from their confines out on stretchers to the ambulances outside.

Where once the horror had been obscured by shadow, then red light, now everything could be seen in bright clarity. The straps. The restraints. The chains. The bloody pools. The piles of human waste. The cages. The needles. The blades. The wire. Every sick device Captain Howdy had for his purpose was laid bare for all to see, catalogue and keep as evidence.

Robbins stood at the edge of the room, staring in, unable to comprehend the sheer horror that happened here. In Helvertown of all places.

"From what we can tell, the victims are from all over the state," Steve said quietly behind him. "Earliest one we can see is three months. It's hard to believe that any of them survived this for so long."

Robbins didn't take his eyes off the room.

"All except Tiana Moore."

"Yeah." Steve nodded slowly. "What that man did here . . . I don't know how these kids can begin to get over it."

Robbins shook his head. "They're not kids anymore," he replied mournfully.

CHAPTER 7

THE SICKNESS

THREE YEARS LATER

The Helvertown State Psychiatric Facility sat eighty miles from the city limits of Helvertown. It housed individuals from across the county who, by reason of mental incapacity, had been found unfit for traditional life, placed instead under clinical care. Most of these individuals were criminals, whose justice for their crimes had been yielded to medical treatment.

Beyond the lush gardens surrounding the facility, the walls inside were thick, the windows all reinforced, every door magnetically locked. This was not merely a hospital but also a maximum-security facility.

Dr. Marion Richter was in her office. She was the facility manager and one who made sure she was involved in every decision. Not micromanagement in her eyes, oversight.

Her hands were clasped together and rested on the desk. Her eyes stayed fixed on the man in the chair across from her.

Dr. Able Calder wore a tweed jacket that hadn't been updated in twenty years. His glasses were thick and sat low on his nose as his overgrown eyebrows stuck out like bushes over the lenses. He held a pen, tapping it softly against the folder on his lap. He wasn't looking at any of the pages inside, didn't need to. He had not only written them, but he had also studied them enough to recite any part from memory.

"I just want your professional opinion, Doctor," Richter said. "I want to hear it from you. Not just a rehash of your report. I need to hear you. What you've suggested, if approved, could become quite controversial."

Calder nodded. "I fully understand that."

He opened the file, which was more of a prop. He did not look down at the words as he spoke. "I can state with utmost certainty that Carleton Hendricks is not the monster he was."

Richter leaned forward. "You mention childhood trauma as a cause? Can you elaborate?"

He didn't answer immediately. Instead, he pulled a paper-clipped collection of papers from beneath the folder and handed it across.

"These are scans of the diary the police found at the scene. Carleton's diary."

She took the pages and glanced through what were photocopied pages of children's handwriting.

"I've read hundreds of histories," he continued. "Psych evaluations, child abuse reports, criminal confessions. But this one? This is the worst case of nonsexual parental abuse I've ever encountered. When we found the diary, Carleton had no memory of any of it. He had shut it out. Over the three years of treatment, we've managed to uncover the trauma he held onto. That he had suppressed without even realizing it. The trauma that caused a split in his psyche. That created the Captain Howdy persona."

"What happened to him?"

"His father was a Marine. Decorated," he sighed. "A very devout man. But Old-Testament devout. Obsessed with discipline but also . . . he didn't seem to want a child. He wanted a soldier. And he tried to make Carleton into one from birth. From what we can tell, the man was completely devoid of empathy or pity. Something that also manifested in the Captain Howdy persona. As if it were a mimic of his father."

Richter scanned more of the pages, still listening.

Calder continued. "He was punished before he could even speak. He was beaten for crying. Deprived of food under the guise as 'training.' Held under bathwater for too long. Made to stand at attention for hours as soon as he was able to. The father treated his son like a broken recruit."

"Was all of this garnered through these pages?"

"No, they just alluded to it all. We used hypnosis and regression therapy."

"And the mother? Was she alive?"

"Yes. And she watched. Never stepped in. Never left. Just let it happen. She was possibly too afraid of her husband, and she died when he was two. That is when the punishments against Carleton got much worse."

Richter sat back, processing. "It may explain but doesn't excuse. So, why are you recommending release?"

"Not an excuse at all," Calder said. "But it explains what he *lost*. His ability to feel anything for others. The wiring in his brain got ripped out and changed. He didn't learn how to be kind. He learned to experience pain without flinching. And when he couldn't cope with it internally, he externalized it as his personality split. When he found tattoos and piercing, it started to build an altar. His father manifested in a new exaggerated form. And that altar became dominant. The real Carleton was shut out of his consciousness. And we have managed to change that through medication and therapy. He does not have access to that sickness in his mind anymore."

Richter stared down at the desk. "If the board approves this release, we will get heat from the public and the press. We will have to justify ourselves. There is no room for error here."

Calder nodded. "I know. But this isn't about us . . . After a lot of work, Carleton Hendrick is finally back in control. Medicated. Cooperative. We cannot continue to punish Carleton for something he had no control over. Especially as that side is gone. But, of course, I see how others will view it, considering all he did."

The small light in the cell had been turned out hours ago. The padded room was quiet, but that did not stop the sounds of the building outside from bleeding in. Somewhere nearby, a door opened and then closed. A shuffling of feet could be heard. Distant conversations. Patients howling in varying states of mania. In this place, there was never a moment of true silence.

Carleton Hendricks lay on his bunk, motionless under a thin white blanket. His eyes were closed. He was asleep. But his mind was in fit of anguish.

Carleton lay on the floor.

He was smaller. Much smaller. The skin on his arms were pale and soft, unblemished by ink and unpierced by metal. He had no clothes and was lying on a bare countertop. It felt cold beneath him. So cold that it was painful.

Around the room was very white and so bright it stung his young eyes.

He was crying. But not screaming or flailing. His whines came from inside in short, sharp bursts. He couldn't control it happening, but even so young, he was trying. The first thing he had ever learned was that crying only made everything hurt more.

Then the footsteps came.

Heavy. Ominous.

This made any effort to quell his torment almost impossible to silence.

That man crouched beside him. Tall. Dressed in a military uniform. The sleeves of his shirt were rolled up to his elbows. A tattoo on his forearm above a thick watch read *Semper Fi*.

The man reached into the front pocket of his shirt and took something out. It was small. Silver. A diaper pin.

The man's hand didn't shake as the point of the pin was pressed against the young Carleton's thigh. Not enough to break skin. Not yet.

As he kicked out to stop what was happening, the hand just pushed the pin in harder.

The baby screamed.

The man's voice followed. Clear, loud and very angry.

"Stop that damn noise, soldier!"

Carleton didn't stop. He couldn't.

The pin went in deeper into his barely formed muscle.

The tears soon turned into gasping wails.

Another pin was brought out.

It scratched at the child's arm this time.

The voice got louder.

"You wanna cry? There's no space for crying in here. Pain is the enemy, soldier!"

More pressure. The second pin broke the skin on his bicep.

The sound of the baby's cries became hoarse as the sobs were broken by sharp inhales.

"You think the enemy cares how you feel?"

The man leaned in closer, his face inches from his child's. His breath reeked with a mix of bourbon and cigars, and his words were cruel.

"Soldiers don't cry. Soldiers don't scream . . . The more noise you make, the worse this'll get."

Of course, the baby did not understand such a threat.

"Fine . . . This is on you."

He jabbed the pin again. This time, through the baby's soft, plump cheek.

"*NO TEARS!*" the man bellowed again, losing any patience he had.

From across the room, a woman stood, watching.

She didn't move. She didn't look away. She didn't even look sad. She just looked blank. She did nothing.

Carleton Hendricks jerked awake.

His eyes shot open.

The nightmare had passed, but his memories of it hadn't.

He stared up at the ceiling, wide awake, the sound of his father's voice still echoing in his mind.

NO TEARS!

He had not thought of his father in so long. But since being here, since the therapy, the past had returned. And every night, he was faced with flashes of it, the explanation of the man he had become but not the excuse. He knew full well what the sickness in him was, and he hated it. Hated what he did. Hated what he put others through.

He closed his eyes but did not sleep. He just lay there until morning.

———

The sun threw thin beams of light through the barred window and across the cell floor, where Carleton sat cross-legged, facing a blank wall, his eyes closed in meditation.

In the hallway, a guard looked in through the reinforced glass of the cell. "Why does he do that?" he asked. "Just sit still like that . . . for hours."

Dr. Calder was behind him, clipboard tucked under his arm.

"He's not sitting," he said. "He's processing."

The guard shrugged, unlocking the door. "Sure looks like a sitting to me."

As Calder stepped into the cell, Carleton's head turned slightly, though not enough to see who it was who entered. He knew, though. He could always smell the doctor's aftershave as soon as he came close.

"Hello, Doctor," he said quietly.

"Do you mind if we talk?"

Carleton nodded as he turned.

The doctor sat on the edge of the bed as the door clanked shut again.

"I had that dream again last night," Carleton said, looking and sounding weak. "They just won't stop, Doc."

"You're starting to work through those memories. That's a good thing. Nightmares are just your brain working its issues out."

Carleton gestured toward his head with two fingers.

"I spent thirty years blocking him out of here. Now, his voice is louder than it's ever been."

"What's he saying?"

Carleton paused. "Nothing new."

"But the fact you can see all this proves you are healing. You are not broken anymore."

Carleton nodded. "I was broken by him," he said. "And he gave the world the pieces."

The doctor smiled kindly. "Carleton, you are a product of cruelty. But now that you see why, you are ready to face the world again. Face the past. Face your ghosts, then move on . . . But . . . can I ask . . . Does your release make you happy?"

Carleton looked at the doctor, then to the floor. "I know I used to believe pain was a tool. That it could free you. Enlighten you," he said. "It was all I knew. Because it's all I had . . . So, now that's gone . . . when I am out . . . what do I have?"

"What do you mean?"

"I'm don't deserve forgiveness—I know that," he said. "But when I'm out. What do I do? Who am I?"

———

The day lit the manicured grounds of the Helvertown State Psychiatric Facility like any other clear spring afternoon. Trees swayed lightly, birds jumped between branches, and the grass below lay neatly trimmed.

Uniformed security dotted the edges of these high-walled gardens. Cameras tracked all motion across it. It seemed calm only if you didn't look beyond the serenity. Though from the cold concrete of a prison, it still had armed guards keeping order and razor wire topping the perimeter walls.

Carleton walked alone along the path that curved by the east side of the building. He moved slowly, hands clasped behind his back, eyes forward but distant. His hair, grown out to its natural blonde and neatly tied into a ponytail, swung gently with each step. The makeup that covered his face was convincing. If you didn't know of the vast amount of tattoo ink that lay below the surface, you'd never guess. There was also no metal in his face. No trace of anything that he was, aside from the stretched holes the piercings had left. When he talked, his lips hardly moved, hiding the filed teeth.

As he walked here in a gray chunky cardigan and beige slacks, his look was soft. Harmless. Almost kind. His sickness, Captain Howdy, was far from here.

He looked as close to at peace as his guilt would allow.

In his hand, he clasped a small black bible. Something he had found comfort in. He was not sure if he believed in any God or holy savior, but the teachings in the book resonated with him. Guided him out of some dark days since he woke up from the horror.

Inside, two doctors watched him from behind a reinforced glass window.

"Take a good look," Dr. Hugh Morrison said quietly. He was short and balding, a thick torso stuffed into a too-small lab coat. His hands thrust into the pockets. He was staring at Hendricks with worry, caution and disbelief. "To release a man like this, back into the very community he tore apart . . ." He shook his head. "It's morally questionable, at best. And without constant supervision, there are no guarantees. Calder should *not* have pushed for this."

Beside him stood Dr. Richter.

"Hendricks passed every benchmark we set," she said. "That's all the board cared about. So, whether we agree with Dr. Calder's findings doesn't matter. The decision's been taken out of our hands."

As they turned from the window and walked toward the administration wing, Morrison's tone didn't soften.

"This is a mistake—you know that, don't you? Three years is not long enough to treat a case like his . . . There *must* be something you can do as director?"

"The law doesn't care about what we think," Richter said. "Only what we can prove. And Dr. Calder has proved what he had to. If it ends badly, it will be on his shoulders, not ours."

———

Genevieve pushed open the front door of her house, kicking it closed behind her with a slam. Her bag hit the floor. She hung up her coat and dropped the house keys in the dish on the sideboard.

Her hair was shorter, cut tight around her face. The color had gone from black to brown. She wore no eyeliner nor jewelry. Her clothes were plain: jeans, sweater, flats. She was no longer the girl she was. Not the girl who rebelled from teenage angst. She was demure. Quiet. Reserved.

"Mom? Dad?" she called out, moving into the empty living room. "I'm home."

Silence.

She had come back from college to visit, as she did every weekend, but usually, her parents would be here waiting for her.

She shrugged and walked across to the couch, thinking nothing more of it.

A voice drifted in from behind her. A deep, malevolent voice.

"The act of slow piercing," it said, "is a transcendent, spiritual event."

Genevieve turned, the words cutting into her mind. Tearing her thoughts apart.

"There is no pain," the voice continued. "Only sensation."

From the bottom of her lungs, she could not hold back the scream that came out of her.

In a panic, she bolted to the left, feet scrambling

beneath her as she tore out of the other side of the living room, through to the kitchen.

"*HELP!*" she cried out. "Mom! Dad!"

The voice behind her followed relentlessly. The words sounded as they came from inside her mind.

"You observe the body as it experiences. You separate the part of you that thinks from the part that the body feels. Stand away from it and appreciate its divinity."

Genevieve reached the staircase and ran up. Getting to her bedroom, she hurled herself inside, shutting it behind her and fumbling at the lock. But as she realized the lock had disappeared, before she could question it, she was yanked backward. Pulled off her feet by an intense and unseen force, her body was launched across the room, and she landed hard upon the bed.

She tried to fight. She tried to scream again.

But rough hands forced her down, then wrenched her around, onto her front.

"Surrender to the experience," the voice continued, calm, measured and too close. "Feel the endorphin rush. The purity of your nerves reacting. The steel slicing through."

Genevieve cried out.

"DAAADDDDYYY HELP ME!!"

The bedroom door immediately burst open as Mike ran inside, followed by Toni. Both carried a look of worry.

"Genny!" he called out.

She was on her bed, thrashing under her covers, her mouth wide as she sobbed.

There was no Captain Howdy. Only sweat. Fear. Tears and the terrible haunting nightmares.

Mike pulled her upright, cradling her close as she cried against his chest.

"It's okay, baby," he whispered. "I'm here. Shhh. Nobody's gonna hurt you. Nobody."

Toni was standing in the doorway. Her eyes were on her daughter and husband as she couldn't help but smile. Half in relief, half in joy that, even with the night terrors and the memories, Genevieve was still alive and coping better than most. She was away at college, rooming with friends in a house in a gated community. One that had guards. The safest place they could find. And she was seemingly happy again as much as she could be. It was just the nightmares that remained.

"No one will ever hurt you again," Mike whispered to her.

———

Today was the day.

Carleton Hendricks sat in his cell in a plastic chair, a bible open on his lap. With a pair of round glasses perched on his nose and his makeup carefully applied, he silently read.

Behind him, his door opened without a knock.

Sam, an orderly, stepped inside. In his mid-twenties,

round and perpetually smiling, he was the kind of person who was made for this job.

"Hey, my man, you ready to rock and roll?" he asked with his usual joviality.

Carleton peered up from his book with a small smile. "Hey, Sam."

"The big day's finally here, dude. You're going home, and, what . . . you're sitting here with your nose in a book? You should be standing by the exit waiting!"

Hendricks marked his page and closed the book. "'I have withdrawn myself from the confusions of cities and multitudes,'" he said. "'And spend my days surrounded by wise books. Bright windows in this life of ours. Lit by the shining souls of men.'"

Sam chuckled. "That one yours? A Carleton Hendricks special?"

"I *wish*," Carleton laughed. "H.G. Wells."

"Well, what's that book there got to say about you going home today?"

Carleton hesitated. His voice dropped a little. "Nothing, really . . . I'm . . . I'm a little nervous if I'm totally honest with you."

"They wouldn't be letting you go if they didn't think you were ready," Sam said. "Just keep up with your meds, keep the therapy schedule, and you'll be fine. I know you will." He gestured outside. "Let's get out of here, huh? The wide world awaits you."

Slowly Carleton got to his feet and reached over to his bed, where a woolen coat lay and put it on.

"Hey, Carleton. Before we go, I should probably let

you know, there's a bit of a . . . welcoming committee at your house."

"I can imagine," Carleton replied sadly.

Sam's picked up Carleton's bag that sat by the door. "No, dude," he said. "I don't think you can. I saw it on the news. Looks like a circus out there."

———

The internal gates of the psychiatric facility clanked open.

Carleton stood, holding his bag close to his chest. The wind rustled the collar of his coat as he took a steadying breath in. Trying to make peace with what was about to happen.

Even he did not believe he was ready for this, but like some of the people here, he had no choice. Doctor Calder and the board said he was ready for reintegration, so he had to believe that they knew what they were talking about.

He closed his mouth, hiding his sharp teeth, then waited for his ride to arrive.

———

The colonial-style home on Harrow Street had changed in appearance over the three years as much as Carleton Hendricks had. No longer a pristine home, it looked more like a crack den from the worst suburb in the worst city. The flowers and once-perfect lawn were all dead. Windows had been smashed and were boarded up. Spray-painted slurs and threats covered the once pristine walls.

Murderer.

Evil.

Satan.

All pained insults scrawled in a defacing rage.

The street outside the house wasn't just crowded but was swollen with every kind of curiosity, outrage, and camera lens. News vans parked along the roads, their antennas rising toward the low sky, their microphones held by the reporters ready. Waiting like vultures for the man of the hour to come home.

Protesters shoved shoulder to shoulder, each louder than the next. Some with signs, others just with fists and rage. The slogans were varied but held the same hatred.

CASTRATION FOR DEFAMATION!

LOCK HIM UP OR HANG 'EM HIGH!

HOW MANY MORE MUST SUFFER?

The chants were as stern as their signs.

"Howdy coming home?" one shouted.

"HELL NO!" came the response.

"Howdy coming home?"

"HELL NO!"

At the center of it all, one woman roared louder than the others. A bullhorn in her hand and flame-colored hair that framed her intense expression of rage. Kathy "Sunny" Macintosh. She had the intense passion of a match about to catch.

"Howdy coming home?"

"HELL NO!"

Across from this crowd, stood another who shouted just as hard, though fewer in number. With tattooed skin. Pierced cheeks. Branded forearms. It was a tribe of body art faithfuls waving signs of their own, throwing their voices back at the ones calling them monsters. They were not counter protesting about Carleton Hendricks but about their community's vilification.

"Short is the pain! Long is the ornament!" they shouted back. Words that meant a lot to them but little to anyone else. "Short is the pain! Long is the ornament!"

The air stung with the kind of tension you don't need to understand to feel.

At the curb, a woman in a tailored blazer adjusted her mic, looking directly into a camera lens. Carol Anne Chalmers-Perez, reporter, smoothed her hair with her palm. Next to her, Jake Hadstrom, her cameraman, had the slow energy of someone who'd been doing this too long and was not fazed by any of it.

Behind her stood a large, shaved-headed and heavily pierced and tattooed man. The man she was about to interview.

Carol Anne whispered to Jake, "Low angles. Get him in frame. I want him looking like he eats glass and punches kittens . . . Like he's a real monster. Okay?"

Jake nodded, not caring either way and just filming it how he wanted to.

She stood up straight and stepped back beside the man. "Okay, count me in," she said.

Jake held up his hand, motioning a silent countdown.

Five.

Four.

Three.

Two.

One.

The red light on the camera blinked on as Carol Anne's smile turned on.

"Welcome back to this special edition of 'Street Talk.' I'm Carol Anne Chalmers-Perez, and we are live outside the home of Carleton Hendricks, aka Captain Howdy, along with many concerned citizens." Her voice was butter smooth. "Only three years ago, Hendricks was convicted of the kidnapping and torture of seven individuals as well as the death of a sixteen-year-old girl, Tiana Moore. Today, he is being released . . . We all have the same questions. Why is he being released? Why back into the exact same house he committed the crimes?"

The camera panned slightly as she motioned to her side. "With me now is Rage, a piercing and branding expert from Agony and Ecstasy, a shop catering to this community, offering tattoos, piercing, and clothing. He is here today with many other body art advocates, protesting this release as well. They believe Hendricks's crimes have painted them in a bad light. Misrepresenting the intentions of the average body-modification enthusiast. What do you have to say, Rage?"

Rage nodded. "Thank you, Carol Anne. The community has been trying for years to erase the image of us as freaks, sickos, psychopaths. We come from all walks of life and enjoy this form of self-expression. I've pierced, branded, and cut everyone from bikers to judges . . . We want everyone to see that this sick bastard was not one of us. What he did wasn't art. It wasn't expression. It was abuse."

Carol Anne stayed poised. "But to the outsider, the difference isn't always clear. What did he do to others that you don't do to yourselves?"

"Consent," Rage replied. "Consent is *everything*. We do this with trust. We don't drug and torture people for kicks. This man broke every principle we live by. Captain Howdy performed these acts on people involuntarily, with the intent to cause pain and suffering for *his* pleasure. This goes completely against our philosophy."

"And your philosophy is what?"

Rage didn't hesitate. "To beautify and elevate our consciousness, through a return to ancient rituals and customs."

Jake's shoulders shook with a suppressed chuckle, finding it all far too pompous.

Carol Anne, meanwhile, had caught a movement in her periphery . . . Something stood beyond the crowd.

"Excuse me, Rage," she said as she grabbed Jake's

shoulder and pulled him and his camera over to a grassy area on the other side of the street.

Detective Mike Gage was there in sunglasses, not saying a word. Just watching the proceedings.

Carol Anne moved toward him, camera pointed.

"Detective Gage," she called out. "Do you have comment on Carleton Hendricks's release? Any feelings you want to share?"

"No comment."

"How do you feel about him being released back into the same house your daughter was tortured in?"

He did not reply, but his jaw clenched, holding back the anger he felt at hearing that.

Carol Anne was about to press on when—

"Here he comes," Jake whispered to her.

His camera spun around as a police cruiser rolled in slowly, with windows tinted, shielding the subject inside from the world. The crowd moved around the vehicle like water around a rock, swarming around it. Letting it pass but slowing it down, screaming and waving their protest signs.

Sunny was the first to reach the passenger-side window, her bullhorn pressed up to the glass. "My Lord, Jesus Christ, will see you burn in hell, you sorry son of a whore!"

Hendricks sat in the back seat. Staring out through the dark glass. His expression was forlorn and very worried.

. . .

A tall man with too much limb and too little sense, Jackson Roth, was on the other side of the car. He slammed a foot into the rear door, then hit it with a fist.

"You don't deserve to be breathing, you piece of shit!" he spat at the glass.

The crowd followed. Screaming. Spitting. Pushing.

The cruiser rocked under the assault.

A nearby group of officers were on hand as they rushed forward and wrestled the baying mob, pushing them back until the cruiser could break free and roll up the driveway of the colonial-style house.

Inside, Carleton Hendricks had been sitting between two uniformed officers. Across from him was Wade Forester, his defense attorney, dressed in a suit worth more than most people's monthly wage.

"Can you handle this, Carleton?" Forester asked.

"I guess it's more can *they* handle it," Hendricks replied meekly, trying to put on a brave face.

Forester nodded as he looked at the officers. "All right, gentlemen, shall we?"

The car doors opened, and as they did, camera flashes erupted in droves. Reporters could not hold back as they barked questions from all sides.

"How does it feel to be free?"

"Do you feel justice was served?"

"How do you sleep at night?"

"Please," Forester said loudly. "Mr. Hendricks has served his time. The state has cleared him to come back into society. He is not here to debate his past, okay? Mr.

Hendricks is trying to make a difficult transition here. You're hounding him—"

"Do you think it's fair that you walk free while a young girl lies dead in her grave?"

Forester persisted in the defense. "The courts made their ruling and found Mr. Hendricks not guilty on medical grounds. He has been treated and released. Now, please, let him get on with his life. He has nothing to say."

But ahead, Carleton stopped at the top step. He turned. His eyes met the angry faces in the crowd.

"I do have something to say," he said quietly. "I do."

He paused as he swallowed, trying to summon the bravery to speak.

The crowd hushed.

"I'm so sorry" was all he could muster.

Everyone heard him.

But nobody believed him.

After saying goodbye to his lawyer and the police escorts, Carleton closed the door behind him, letting the bolt click into place as if it were a punctuation to that moment. The click sounded, and he finally felt able to breathe. The murmured voices of the reporters still pressed against the outside, shouting their questions to the house, but he didn't dare go out there to speak. He didn't even turn to look out of the window. He could hear them well enough to know that hate was out there. He could hear the protests. Even though he believed he deserved to go out there and face their wraith, he could not endure the confrontation.

He stood against the door, his shoulder resting lightly against the wood. Slowly, he turned around and looked through the peephole. Beyond the fish-eyed lens, officers had begun to disperse the crowds. Reporters, stubborn and hungry, did not appreciate being moved further back and tried to shout through it, asking the same questions. But within a few minutes, the collected volume had started to lower as the crowd thinned out. The protesters, not knowing what more they could do, decided to leave.

Twenty minutes later, Carleton was still there, peering out.

The street was empty aside from the policemen waited till the last person left, hanging around a while longer before heading back to the station.

He let out a sigh of relief as he finally stepped away from the door and turned to face what had become of his house.

He switched the lights on. Surprisingly, they still worked, and they shone over the devastation that had been wrought since he had been arrested. The house had been locked and boarded up, but that did not stop those who were intent of getting in. Kids, the curious, junkies, all fought their way in here and left their marks.

In all of the rooms he wondered through, furniture had been overturned, ripped apart. Spray paint coated almost every wall in thick, angry slogans and signs. Some of what had been written were words, others drawings, others just tags. It seemed that every surface throughout the house was vandalized or violated in some way.

The drywall throughout had been punched over multiple points, revealing the insulation and brickwork beneath. In one room, charred streaks ran up from where they had clearly tried and failed to set fire to the building. Bottles were shattered across the floors, leaving blankets of broken glass wherever he went. Trash was also left everywhere. Old food containers, wrappers, remnants of parties. Old puddles of sick and urine where people were caught short. It did not stop there, as, lying in what had once been his bedroom, a large mound of human waste sat, steaming on the warped floorboards. Not left from one person but many. And not left through necessity. It was a clear message.

Carleton didn't move. Didn't react. He just stared at it. He expected a lot but not this. This was a surprise.

Then, slowly, deliberately, he closed his eyes and drew in a slow and steady breath. This one deeper and calming as he forced himself to think. They were acting out their justified anger against him—he knew that. He just needed to accept it humbly. That is what the bible said. And God or no God, the lessons were right.

He had found a broom in a closet, and his lawyer had brought supplies like toilet paper and trash bags, so he resigned himself to the fact that cleaning this house was just a tiny piece of his penance.

CHAPTER 8

STREET JUSTICE

Color bloomed as a dozen hot air balloons, tethered and swaying in place, filled the field with their massive bulks. Some were just beginning to take off as their burners erupted with hisses. Others stayed still, full and ready, anchored in wait, hovering just above the grass.

The fairground behind them had been open since morning and was already crowded, filled with families having fun in the spring sunshine. They walked between the fairground booths, with children running around with cotton candy stuck to their faces. The gentle breeze carried with it a strong smell of popcorn and sugar.

Mike Gage wore sunglasses and a ball cap low on his brow as he walked with his hands in his jacket pockets. Toni was beside him, and for the first time in years, she looked more like herself again. The smile she wore wasn't forced. It looked gentle, natural, as if joy had finally made its way back to her life. She had laughed at something Genevieve had said, then brushed the back of her hand against Mike's arm like it was habit. It was familiar. It was safe. It was happy. Not that the marriage had been fixed, but it had become more comfortable since they got their daughter back from the hospital.

Genevieve walked just ahead of them, telling them about her time away at college. As she spoke, the wind blew at her hair as she squinted up at one of the balloons already lifting into the sky. With no makeup, and no trace of her angst, her steps seemed lighter than they ever had before. She walked with ease, and her voice had a trace of the fun-loving person she once had been.

"And my new professor is just *impossible* to understand," she said, launching into her complaint without looking back. "Every sentence trails off at the end like someone is lowering his volume. He's like . . ." She cleared her throat and dropped her voice into a dull monotone. "'Everyone, please take out your books and turn to page . . .'" The words dissolved into a mumble. "'There will be a test next Friday on the . . .'" Again, her voice disappeared into nothing.

Toni laughed loudly. Genevieve looked back cracked a grin, proud of the impersonation.

Mike didn't say anything. He was too lost in his own thoughts.

"Mike," Toni said, noticing his distraction and nudging his arm playfully. "That reminds me of the teacher you had who wrote on the blackboard with his right hand and erased what he had just written with his left. Remember?"

He didn't smile. He didn't even hear what she said. He was too distracted.

"It's not right," he said under his breath.

"What? That he was left-handed?"

"They just let him out?" Mike said, hurt and annoyed, as if the words had been sitting too long and soured before they made their way over his lips.

Toni stopped smiling. Her brightness dulled as she leaned a little closer, knowing what he was talking about and not wanting Genevieve to hear.

"Het," she said quietly, "don't let him take any more of our lives, okay? You did your job. All by the book." She squeezed his arm reassuringly. "Gen's okay . . . We're all okay. We're here right now, a family. Together!"

"A chemical imbalance?" he replied bitterly, again ignoring her words. "It's a fucking excuse."

Toni turned fully toward him, slowing him down. "Mike, we've been together too long . . ." She tried to soften her words. Needing to reach him. "You're starting to sound as negative as my mom."

Neither of them has seen Genevieve stop and turn, hearing what was said.

She walked back over to her parents and spoke with more weight than her age should have allowed. "Dad," she said, "I love you for caring so much about me, but I'm okay. I'm dealing with it. It's not your pain to carry, okay? We just all have to move on, or we won't be living our lives. We will be trapped in them."

Before he could answer, a new voice was heard.

"Listen. Just because we're partners doesn't mean we have to do *everything* together. Sheesh, it's like you're stalking me!"

Detective Christian walked over the field toward them, his sunglasses hanging from his shirt collar, his smile already halfway to sarcastic. Beside him, his new girlfriend, Faith, walked quietly beside him. The two of them approached with the ease of people used to interrupting.

Everyone exchanged hellos, a few smiles, though Mike's was more of a twitch than a gesture. His mind was still on Carleton Hendricks, dwelling in places the sun did not reach.

Steve looked him over once and raised an eyebrow. "So, what's got that big brain of yours in overdrive, huh?"

Toni didn't even hesitate. "What do you think?"

Steve sighed. "Yeah, I'm having trouble with that one myself."

"It's just not fucking right," Mike said. "I gotta go."

He didn't wait for a response. He stepped away as he walked toward the far end of the field.

Toni, Genevieve, Steve and Faith watched him go.

Steve was the first to speak.

"Man, he needs to stop. This shit will consume him."

"Yeah, he has to move in," Genevieve replied casually, much to the surprise of her mother.

———

The night swallowed Helvertown as dark clouds came in without warning, pressing heavy across the town as if it knew that an unwelcome presence had returned. As if the angry mood of the people had summoned the storms, it ended the warm spell in less than a week after Hendrick's return.

In a rent-controlled house within spitting distance of the railroad, the kitchen was clean. Too clean. Uncomfortably clean. Every surface had already been wiped down multiple times and was being wiped down yet again. Madeline Roth moved in small, anxious circles around the room. Her hands busied themselves with the sponge and bleach spray, even though there was no dirt left to chase.

From the living room, the television played the nightly news. The anchor's voice was turned loud and sounded as if they were speaking in the room.

"Today's protests were endemic of the growing resentment to the judicial process. With Carleton Hendricks being deemed mentally incapable of his crimes and being released last week, the question stands, was justice actually served?"

Madeline heard but didn't actually listen to any of the words. She was too concerned with not upsetting her husband. She was petite, almost mouse-like, with thin features and a voice that rarely rose above conversational. And tonight, her nerves were strung so tightly that they made her fingers tremble. Every time she glanced at the clock, her eyes darted back to the cleaning at hand.

Jackson Roth stood across the room from her, leaning against the sink, staring at her sternly. He was still dressed in his work attire: stained jeans, a faded flannel shirt, with his hair shadowing his sour expression. His beer was already half-empty, and he, too, hadn't stopped glaring at the clock since the game was interrupted by a news report.

"Where the fuck is she?" he said angrily.

Madeline jumped a little at his tone but tried not to show it. "She—she's probably just at a friend's, I bet—"

"I'll *tell* you where she is," Jackson snapped drunkenly back, pointing his bottle toward the window. "Out humpin' some random guy . . . Like mother, like daughter."

"I'm sure she'll be back soon," Madeline said, swallowing any trace of her own worry. "Probably just lost track of the time, that's all."

Jackson stared at his wife as if she were the cause of not just how their daughter acted but for all the ills in his life. Just as he always did. If he had a bad day at work, it was her fault. If the Mets lost, her fault.

From the TV, the newscaster was still speaking loudly.

"In case you're just joining us, the controversy still rages over the release of a potentially dangerous man from the Helvertown State Psychiatric Facility. Earlier this week. Carleton Hendricks, better known as Captain Howdy, has parents and concerned citizens protesting at his discharge not just back into the Helvertown community but into the very house he committed the crimes in."

Jackson's ears pricked up, hearing what was said.

His beer bottle raised slowly to his lips as he took a swig, but he didn't stop until he downed it all.

———

The neon sign outside the Moorside Motel blinked *Vacancy*. Beneath it, another line of text had been written, hand-painted and sun-faded: *Hourly Rates Available*.

The building was a one-story row of rooms with peeling paint and rotten wood. The sort of establishment that only took cash, and no one made eye contact.

Inside Room 6, the lights were dimmed as low as they could go without switching off. The heavy mothballed curtains were drawn, blotting out the streetlight that sat outside. On the rickety bed, underneath the musty stained sheets, two teenagers lay tangled in clumsy sexual aftershock.

Garrett Russell was on his back, chest heaving, eyes closed, drops of sweat dripping down his forehead. His mouth was open, reaching for breath as he was unable to hide his satisfaction.

Beside him was Kelly Roth. She wasn't out of breath. She was barely even flushed. Her makeup was intact, and she looked as if she had just lain down. She turned and looked at Garrett like he was a lab experiment that had failed to meet even the most basic of expectations.

He let out a heavy sigh and shifted to one side, already falling toward sleep.

Seeing this, Kelly nudged him with her elbow. "Garrett," she said, "don't you dare pass out on me."

He didn't answer coherently. He just mumbled, barely audibly.

"I've gotta be home by midnight," she added, "or my dad'll freak the fuck out."

Garrett made another noise, maybe an agreement, maybe a loving pleasantry . . . She didn't know . . . or even care.

She turned to the digital clock on the nightstand. The orange numbers shone 23:21.

"I'm gonna wake you in, like, a half-hour, all right?"

But Garrett was already fast asleep.

She stared up into the shadows above the bed. She felt numb, not from pleasure but from the weight of what would come next: the ride home, the excuses, her dad screaming at her like a machine gun.

But for now, this motel room was peaceful. She would enjoy it for as long as she could.

Outside, the sound of thunder cracked high in the sky.

———

Jackson wrenched open the refrigerator door again. The light spilled onto his face, accentuating every angry line. He reached in, fumbled with one hand and came out with his seventh beer of the evening. The bottle cap fell and clinked to the linoleum floor. He did not pick it up nor care about making a mess.

"What about that piece of shit, huh?" Jackson slurred. His voice had that edge to it. The low gravel that signaled he was crossing from drunk to dangerous, an edge that made Madeline nervously tense. "You heard the news. That freak is back on the streets. And if . . . If he's got her . . ." He just stared at the doorway, past his wife, like he could see the man through the walls.

He downed that bottle in one sitting, then staggered back to the fridge for another.

Madeline wondered what she could say to stop this. The sponge was still held limp in her hand as she slowly wiped the table. Her mouth opened, shut again, then opened once more with careful hesitation.

"Jackson . . . Honey, are you sure you want to have another beer? I'm sure Kelly's all right. She's—"

Jackson whirled toward her. No words, no gestures. And it was enough to make her flinch. She had been with him too long to not know what was coming.

Each one of his words was aimed at her, sharp and full of blame. "Some psychotic prick may have our daughter, and you just say she's all right?" He pointed the neck of the new beer bottle like it was a knife. "And who the fuck are *you* to tell me I've had enough to drink? This is my fuckin' house. My fuckin' fridge. My fucking world that I allow you to live in."

He strode over to her, leaving the fridge wide open, and raised his hand.

Madeline shrank back instinctively. She knew better than to stand up for herself or say another word.

But he did not hit her. His hand froze before he smirked to himself. Pleased with his abusive control over her.

"Give me the goddamn phone," he sneered.

She nodded quickly, obediently. The cordless receiver clicked off its cradle on the wall, and she offered it to him like it was the most fragile thing in the world.

"I . . . I can call the police," she said, not quite sure what the right thing to say was. "They can find her."

Jackson snatched the phone from her hand. "It's too late for that, you fucking dumb bitch," he said. "They had their chance." His mind was focused on a thought that he was too stupid, too drunk, too ignorant to ignore.

He turned away from her, his thumb already jabbing at the buttons.

"What are you going to do?" she asked.

He paused for half a second before the dial tone clicked into a ring. He didn't look back.

"What should have been done already." Then, into the receiver, with an already satisfied grin, he said, "G-man. It's Jackson. Mount up . . . We'll meet at the bar in thirty, got it? Make some calls. Get the boys." He paused, his grin turning perverse. "And Gene-o? Bring the equipment . . . We got some street justice to hand out."

He handed the phone back to his wife.

She looked at him fearfully as she took it.

Then, with a look of satisfaction, he opened the bottle. Downed half of it, then threw the rest against the wall, smashing it. Sending glass and beer everywhere.

She winced. Not saying a word.

"This place better be fucking spotless when I get back."

———

The colonial-style house on Harrow Street was quiet.

In the dining room, the most untouched room in the house, Carleton Hendricks sat alone. The walls were still daubed in a multitude of cruel slogans, but there was no longer any broken furniture or trash in here. He had spent every day since he had come home cleaning the whole house up. He had gone around taking the boards off the windows and doors at the back of the house. He had scraped black paint off the inside of the glass, once more allowing light into the rooms.

With a chair from another room and a television

playing quietly, he had nothing left to clean or fix. He looked despondent. Lost. He missed the safety of his cell. The certainty of what each day would bring.

Before it happened, he had turned toward the bay windows as a shadow flitted and a sound was heard from outside.

Then all at once, the windows exploded inward. Shattered as if hit by a truck. Followed but a half dozen figures.

The first thing to hit him was the floor as the force pushed him backward off the chair.

Then the other hits followed.

Boards. Bats. Boots.

They had crashed through the ruined frame. All screamed in a drunken rage. The first to reach Carleton was Jackson Roth, who kicked him hard in the ribs as he lay on the ground. Carleton grunted in pain as the boot then slammed into his chin.

"What did you do with her?" Jackson roared. "What the *fuck* did you do with my daughter?"

The others soon joined in, kicking, clawing, shouting. Every voice trying to be louder and more furious than the last, and not one of them were waiting for answers. This was not an inquisition. This was not about his daughter. This was an excuse.

Carleton didn't fight back.

He couldn't.

He wouldn't.

He knew he didn't deserve it.

He understood what was happening to him.

. At first, he tried to shield his head. His arms came up, barely able to move under the sheer weight of battering. But as the boots and hands landed onto his ribs and back and stomach, something in his mind started to shift. To crack.

"This is what happens when slime escapes the law!" one shouted.

"No mercy," shouted another.

"Get him," a third added.

Then Carleton started to detach from the agony, just as he did when he was a small child. Forced to run from the pain in order to survive the ordeal.

Like a door closing inside his mind. He left the torment of his body, abandoning the feeling and locking himself away.

"*Fuck you*!" Jackson screamed as he turned from Carleton, picked up the chair, and smashed it against the wall. The rest of the mob took the cue. One kicked a lamp over. Another hit his bat through the television screen. They didn't need any encouragement.

"*We'll even up the score*!" Jackson shouted through a rictus grin.

Hands then reached down and gripped Carleton from every side.

Dragged him across the floor, through the shards of broken glass and splinters, Carleton felt nothing.

Outside, the mobs' cars and trucks idled with their engines still humming as they ticked over, left on.

Doors still open. Each having been too eager to capture its prey. The rain that poured dulled all the sounds of the chaos bleeding from the back of the colonial-style house.

The mob soon spilled around the corner and onto the lawn, dragging Carleton like a bag of trash. His hands and feet had been bound with cable ties and rope.

He did not resist. He didn't struggle. He didn't scream. The beatings had stopped mattering. And even the fear had drained from his face. He accepted all of what was about to happen, knowing that he would not make it to see another sunrise.

And he was glad.

He kept remembering a line from the bible: *Give justice to the weak.*

Across the street, a car was parked in shadow. Detective Mike Gage watched from inside. Hands on the wheel, eyes on the scene. Witnessing the man who tortured his daughter being kidnapped.

His hand hovered near his radio mic, fingers brushing against it.

He did not know if he could call this in. He knew he should . . . But . . .

As he sat staring, his duty faded into the distance.

Carleton was being slammed against one of the cars, his face slammed sideways against the window. And as if by a strange twist of happenstance, his gaze, through all the darkness and torrential storm, somehow found Mike.

They locked eyes.

Not for long. But something passed between them. Recognition.

Mike stared back.

On the sidewalk behind the car, as Carleton was thrown inside, something had rolled out from of his pants. A small vial. Plastic. Clear. A label with his name. A bottle of medication. It hit the concrete and bounced once before settling in a patch of dead leaves.

The convoy of cars and trucks quickly pulled out, and one by one, their tires crushed the vial. Pills spilled out, crunching to powder under the drunken procession.

And just like that, he was gone. Mike sat there, feeling no relief at all. Not as he thought he should be.

———

The mob continued to drive through the storm along a two-lane road beyond the city limits.

In the lead truck, Jackson sat in the passenger seat beside Gene "G-Man" Gagliardi. Gene was stocky, round in the middle, with a heavily pockmarked face. Behind them, two younger men, Pug and Raf, sat on either side of Carleton, who was slumped in the back seat.

Nobody spoke.

Nobody needed to.

They all knew where this road would end.

Gene glanced in the rearview as Carleton stared right back at him blankly.

"What the fuck are you lookin' at, freak?" Gene snapped.

"Easy there, G-Man. Keep your eyes on the road," Jackson said, not bothering to turn around. "Fucker's done for."

As he spoke, his eyes caught something ahead. He leaned forward in his seat as his mouth fell open. "What the hell . . . ?"

Through the wet windshield, barely visible in the rain, a car sat turned sideways across the road. Two figures were in front of it, waving them down.

Gene saw it and slowed the truck to a stop.

Jackson's confusion turned into something else. He squinted harder and angrier.

"Bitch!" he seethed as he saw them clearly.

His wife, Madeline, and his daughter, Kelly.

Both soaked. Both running toward the car.

Kelly reached the passenger-side window first, her hands pressed to the glass, her voice muffled.

"Daddy, I'm all right! I fell asleep at Heather's house. I'm fine! Please, don't! Stop this!"

Jackson didn't react. He looked to the others in the car. They didn't react either. No one moved.

He rolled down the window and glared at his wife. "Maddy, go home. *Now.*"

"Jack," Madeline pleaded desperately. "She's okay. He didn't take him. You can let him go."

"It's too late for that. Go. Home."

He turned away from them and rolled the window back up.

Gene pressed on the gas, and the car moved forward, edging around Jackson's family. The other vehicles followed, each slowly passing the two soaked women.

Kelly's voice screamed through the rain, after the cars. "*But he didn't do it! I'm all right! He didn't do anything to me!*"

Her words fell to nothing. Ineffectual and ignored.

The hillside came into view not long after they had turned off the freeway. The cars snaked up a small muddy trail that climbed toward the ridge. In the distance, the Helvertown's lights flickered on the horizon.

Up at the clearing, the wind was strong and unrestricted. The rain was battering and relentless. The vehicles parked up one by one beside each other. The headlights left on illuminating a large old tree.

The vigilantes then stepped out, forming a silent march as they pulled Carleton out with them.

As the rain soaked them all to the bone, the makeup covering Carleton's facial tattoos had begun to run, smearing down his face. The inked skin beneath slowly showed his features.

Jackson had taken a rope from the back of one of the trucks, and now flung it over one of the tree's thick branches. The noose at the other end of the rope dropped over and swung down. A group of four, led by Rainer Savitch—a man with only three teeth in his head—took the rope's other end. Ready to take the weight.

The two men holding Carleton dragged him forward and, without a word, fastened the noose around his neck.

Mary Delgado, a cruel-looking woman with a stogie sticking out the side of her mouth, waked over and kicked Carleton hard in the groin. "Die, you frickin' bastard!" she shouted.

Carleton crumpled slightly. He wheezed, but he didn't fall. His eyes closed and mouth began to move. Words came out. Words he had no control over. He looked up at Mary. "The Eskimos have a saying, you know," he said with a quiver of emotion. "'Let the person who wants a vision hang himself by the neck. When his face turns purple, take him down and have him describe what he has seen.'"

He paused and turned toward the men holding the rope. His eyes settled on Rainer.

"There's another saying that I think is quite apt here," Carleton added, raising his voice over the sound of the rain. "'Just fucking do it already.'"

As he spoke, Carleton felt numb. He felt weak. He felt like he was losing grip on something . . .

"*Puuuuuulllll!*" a voice screamed from the shadows.

And the men pulled on the rope without delay. It immediately went taut, lifting Carleton from the ground in one smooth motion.

As his body was hauled upward, his mouth opened, but no sound came as his throat was being crushed.

His still-bound legs kicked out. His body twisted. And as he thrashed, the tree branch above groaned under the strain.

The thunder and lightning crashed high above, accompanying the downpour, hiding the sound of the branch cracking.

Carleton's body jerked harder and harder, convulsing with an immense force. His mind was not trying to stop this, but his body instinctively was.

The branch above creaked more and more as it began to splinter.

The men on the rope had trouble keeping hold, so they quickly tied off the end to the trunk of the tree.

Within a couple of minutes, as they all witnessed the life being lynched out of Carleton Hendricks, everything stopped.

His limbs went still.

His eyes stayed open and empty.

Jackson turned and walked back to the car. Mary, Gene, Rainer and the rest all did the same. No one spoke. Their job was done.

The wind picked up as it moved over the clearing, sweeping across the makeshift gallows where Carleton had been hanged.

As the mob drove away, something was happening at the end of the noose.

Carleton's spirit. His will. His primal need to survive, or whatever part of him still held a speck energy, grew. It rose upward from the depths of his being.

Finally, the branch gave way and snapped under the weight.

Carleton, still bound by the rope and cable ties, fell hard to the ground below as his limbs broke free and his bindings fell apart. He landed chest-first, crushing into the mud as the shock of the impact drove air back into his lungs.

A beat later, his eyes shot open.

Not Carleton's eyes.

A wheeze escaped his throat, jagged and painful.

Not Carleton's throat.

He rolled onto his back, coughing violently, with mud caked across his face. His chest rose and fell with uneven breaths. He was alive.

Not Carleton.

His voice was rough and broken.

"What a rush," Captain Howdy said as he laughed to himself, staring up at the sky with wonder.

———

Tall, ominous trees lined the path that cut through the cemetery.

Through the moonless, murky darkness, a man staggered.

He moved further into the cemetery, between rows of identical graves. White military headstones stretched out in a regiment, names carved upon them in an identical fashion.

The man found what he was looking for and dropped to the ground, his knees hit without grace or resistance.

The headstone before him was familiar.

He stared at it, lips moving with nothing behind them. The rain plastered his long hair to his scalp, the makeup on his face totally washed away.

His hand came down hard on the headstone.

Once.

Twice.

Striking it in anger.

He struck it a third time, this time with both fists. Then again. And again.

The rage burst out of him like bile, sharp and fast, but it had no real aim. The violence wasn't for the man beneath the ground. Not really. It was for everything that led him here.

He was now Captain Howdy, but something had brought him here. Some remnants of Carleton Hendricks screaming from the depths of whatever humanity was left.

Finally spent, his chest heaved as he collapsed forward onto the grave, arms spread, exhausted and emotional. He could not stop himself as the sobs began. From deep inside, broken cries that had been waiting all his lifetime came out.

The gravestone in front of him was a simple one.

Spartan in its lettering. Clean and heartless, like the man buried below.

Bradford Hendricks
April 18th, 1922 – 1994
"The engine is discipline."

Captain Howdy looked down, reading the shadowed words again and again as if they might change.

They didn't.

And as his tears finally ended, so too was the remnants of Carleton Hendricks.

CHAPTER 9

ASCENSION

A week later, the storm had once again left, and the woods around Haverlock Common were bright. The morning sun had touched the horizon and slipped between the trees, casting its gentle hue across the parking lot. Captain Churchill Robbins stood by his car, dressed in pristine jogging gear, moving through various stretches. He may have been in his sixties, but his body was as fitter than ever.

A second vehicle rolled up and parked beside him.

Mike climbed out.

Gray sweatpants, a faded college sweatshirt, off-brand sneakers with well-worn soles, his outfit said he didn't do this kind of thing often.

"Glad you made it," Robbins said. "You need to stretch or anything first?"

Mike didn't hesitate with a smile. "Define 'or anything.'"

"I'll take that as a 'no.'" Robbins laughed. "Shall we?"

———

In a darkened room in an abandoned house, the only light came from a cluster of candles on the floor that fluttered softly.

Open boxes and ripped plastic lay in piles. Packaging of items stolen from the computer store a few days ago. The frontage of which had been smashed with a rock, but only three items had been taken. A laptop, a long stretch of ethernet cable, and a modem. Not even the owner had noticed those items were missing. The police had quickly chalked it up to some vandal kids, smashing for the thrill, then running away, afraid.

The clacking of typing on a keyboard followed the sound of a modem connecting to the internet.

Captain Howdy sat cross-legged on the floor as the screen brightly lit his face. The face that bore its filed teeth in a wide, lascivious grin.

A low, almost animalistic sound escaped him.

Not a word. Closer to a purr. A pleased purr.

———

Through the woods, the trail narrowed as it curled around a collection of large, exposed roots. Branches overhead filtered out most of the light, dappling the path ahead in patches of gray and gold. The only sounds here were the rhythm of running feet and the wheeze of Mike's increasingly labored breathing.

"How far now?" he asked, his voice grasping to form words.

Robbins didn't slow down as he replied. His breathing was in control, his body barely even affected by the exertion. "You're in luck. I'm only doing five miles today. So, let's speed this up."

Robbins was light on his feet as he sped up, and Mike lagged a dozen steps behind. His every stride was effortful as the distance between them widened by the second.

Ahead, the trail evened out as the incline leveled. Mike dug in, pushing himself forward . . . But he suddenly hit the limit and had to stop as he bent double at the waist, hands gripping his knees.

"Dammit, Church!" he called out. "How often do you do this?"

Robbins barely looked winded as he turned, jogging on the spot still.

"I try to get out at least three times a week," he said as his jog slowly stopped. "How about we walk for a bit."

Mike smiled gratefully as he stood up and walked over to him.

Robbins looked ahead down the trail as he spoke. "People always ask me what's the toughest part of my job. You know what I tell them? It's watching other people screw things up."

Mike didn't respond.

"No matter how many times I've seen it, I never get used to watching criminals walk free. The jails are overcrowded. There's insufficient evidence, DNA tests, high-priced defense teams, violation of rights. It's always *something*. But the bottom line is, sometimes, we arrest the bad guys, and they will just go free. Justice isn't just blind—it's also unfair."

Mike nodded slowly, not disagreeing.

Robbins looked over at him again, made sure he was really hearing it.

"*We're* cops. *We're* the good guys. We're not the judge, the lawyer, or the court-appointed psychiatrist. We're not the warden or parole officer. We're not politicians or clergy. We're cops. We arrest bad guys. It's what we do. It's what you do. You do your job the best you can and pray everybody else does theirs. Even if it ends up shit. We do what we can."

They began walking in silence, along the path and toward the clearing where their cars were parked.

Robbins slowed down.

Mike didn't notice at first as he kept on a few steps before realizing he was alone.

He turned.

Robbins looked him dead in the eye.

"This is where it starts. The minute we stop doing our job, the minute we stop being cops, it's over. Because, without arrests, there can be no long, drawn-out trials for high-priced lawyers. They can't wave DNA tests in the faces of lenient judges who give reduced sentences."

He took a breath.

"And reform wardens can't make recommendations to overburdened parole boards to give early release for good behavior to bad pieces of utter shit."

He unclipped a water bottle attached to his waist, took a sip, then handed it to Gage.

"The minute we stop being cops, the minute we stop being the good guys, the whole thing falls apart. It starts with us. You understand?"

Mike nodded. He took the offered bottle, took a gulp and handed it back.

"I get it," he said. "Now, what's this gotta do with me?"

Robbins gave him a long look.

"I'd like to think nothing," he said. "But you *have* to find Carleton Hendricks. We've been asked by his parole officer to open a case, and I am passing it over to you. And I hope, for all our sakes, that he's okay."

"Me?! Why me? Of all people? How is this our department?"

"Because out of everyone we have in the precinct, you're most likely to find him. If he's out there up to his old tricks, you can have the glory of righting a wrong and putting him back in jail. If not, then . . . Then it may prove to you that he has been rehabilitated, no matter how much you or I can't believe it." There was a pause before he continued. "You can start by interviewing Hendricks' neighbor, Mrs. Moskowitz. Says she heard the commotion the night Hendricks's house was broken into and destroyed. Saw a man, in a navy-blue sedan, parked near the house. Watching. You find that guy, share my little speech with him. 'Cause it sounds like he could use it."

Their eyes met briefly.

The point had been made. Robbins knew Mike was there that night. He had given him the case not just for his sake but as a punishment and a lesson and a chance to make things right.

———

The bedroom was bathed in a glow from the television, upon which a hardcore movie played without subtlety.

The sound was loud and the scenes were in extreme close-up.

Jackson sat on the bed, stripped naked, with a throbbing erection. He sat up, restless, stroking his member gently. He wasn't doing that for what was on screen. He was watching it as he kept himself ready, getting more frustrated by the second.

"Maddy, will you come the hell on?" he called out, irritated. "I'm losing my hard-on, for Christ's sakes."

From behind the closed bathroom door, Madeline's answered soft and strained.

"I'll be right there. This stuff isn't easy to put on, you kn—"

Something shattered from within the bathroom.

Jackson sat upright, his grip on his member falling away.

"What are you doing in there? I need you in here.

Now!" he snapped. Then, under his breath, he said, "Dumb fuckin' bitch."

Grimacing and needing his relief, his attention shifted back to the screen. The girl in the video looked so young, and her pained expression lit something inside him that he liked. As the middle-aged man on the screen dominated her, playing out a scene of discipline, it made Jackson feel like finishing this himself and not waiting for his wife.

"That's right." He salivated as he gripped himself again and continued stroking harder. "Give her what she wants."

He barely noticed the bathroom door open.

The funky music from the film started to play loudly as the scene kicked into solely hard thrusting and loud moans.

In the shadow of the doorway, Madeline appeared. Her body glistened faintly in the television light. Dressed in a red corset and fishnet stockings, she also wore red gloves that climbed past her elbows. She had made the effort, just as he demanded. And for a woman so beaten down by abuse, she wore it damn well.

Jackson turned his gaze, and his eyes lit up, his lust turning from the film to her.

"Oh yeah. Come to papa." He sank back in the bed, the film still playing loudly and graphically.

Madeline moved closer, her body swaying, slow yet awkwardly. She swept her arms in wide arcs, wiggling her hips in an off-beat rhythm. Her face was difficult to read in the low light.

Jackson saw none of that. He just saw her as a willing piece of meat that he owned, coming closer for him to have his fun with.

"Damn, Maddy, you're turning me on." He gripped himself harder, pumping faster.

She drifted closer, slowly, still moving, still dancing.

From a distance, it looked like she had a choker around her neck. Thin and dark, resting against her red corset.

Jackson pumped even faster. "All right, enough. Come over here and spread those cheeks."

She didn't answer. She didn't stop dancing either. But her movements grew smaller, more confined as she came right up to him.

"What are you, deaf? Now, bend the fuck ov—" The words fell from his mouth. "*Oh my God!* Maddy, your neck!"

Her throat had been slit wide open. A deep wound, running from one ear to the other. She also wasn't wearing red. It was once white. The blood from her wound flowed down her chest, soaking into her skin and staining what she wore. All of it. The clothes, the gloves, the stockings. Everything was dripping in crimson.

She lunged.

Her body slammed on top of Jackson with horrible force. And as she did, her hands somehow hit against him with a strength she never had in life. The sound was brutal. Bone striking bone, followed by the sickening crunch of her own hands breaking under the impact.

Jackson flailed, shielding himself with his arms.

"Maddy. Stop!"

His eyes then locked on something behind her.

In the shadows stood Captain Howdy.

His eyes were wild, his hair dyed red once more, every piercing put back into place. The make up he once used to cover his identity was in the past.

It wasn't Madeline attacking him. Her body had been held up by Howdy. Strapped to him like a puppet. Her arms bound to his arms. Her legs to his legs. Her body nothing more than a suit of flesh, moved by his will.

He stepped closer. "Wanna play a game?" he said with a giggle as he punched Jackson in the face. Knocking him out with a single blow.

Howdy did not stop there. Despite his victim's unconsciousness, the punches kept coming. He pounded Jackson's face, still with Madeline strapped to him. He punched and punched until Jackson's cheekbones had both shattered, his eye sockets cracking and his nose broken into a pulp.

———

The wipers swung across the windshield with a thumping rhythm.

Kathy "Sunny" Macintosh sat in the passenger seat, annoyed as she perpetually was. Her husband, Peter, was sitting behind the wheel. He was a slight man with soft features and a muscle mass of zero.

He was driving cautiously, keeping both hands on the wheel at ten and two o'clock, just as his instructor told him three decades earlier.

"I don't believe it. Look at that," Sunny moaned, pointing out of the window.

Up ahead, in front of their house, a man stood leaning against a tree. Disheveled. Weathered. A vagrant in a long-battered raincoat wearing a wide-brimmed hat. Around him the rain was pouring, but the man didn't shelter. He just stood in their garden, his back to them.

"A goddamn bum in this neighborhood? Are you kidding me? In front of our house?" She sucked on her teeth. "Pull up now. I'm not letting this stand. Not at all."

Peter hesitated, then quietly obeyed, slowing the car and rolling up onto the driveway.

As the engine stopped, Sunny didn't wait. But she didn't move.

"Get rid of him now!" she commanded.

Peter looked uncomfortable as he stared back out at the homeless man. "Why don't we just call the police? No need for any confrontation."

"We don't need the police. This is our *home*." Sunny spoke like a mother chastising a naughty child. "Now get over there and chase him away."

Peter held his ground. "What if he's g—"

"What if he's *nothing. Get rid of him.*"

Before he considered arguing his point, he knew he had no voice here. She had made up her mind, and he had no choice but to follow her every command.

The driver's side door opened, and he got out into the storm.

Walking uneasily across the drive, he approached the vagrant, who was still standing with his back to them.

Sunny got out of the passenger side, and with her handbag over her head to shield her from the rain, she stared over at her husband.

"Excuse me, sir," Peter said. "Would you mind moving on? It's just my wife—"

He didn't get to finish the sentence.

The vagrant spun around with violent speed and, with a large butcher's knife in his grip, thrust it hard into Peter's chest.

The blade went in fast, deep, and final.

Peter gasped as blood sprayed from his mouth, the knife having slid through his lung and embedded into his spinal cord.

There was no fight here. No struggle. He just dropped to the ground in a heap, and the vagrant retrieved his knife.

The storm ahead masked Sunny's screams.

Her husband's chest wound gaped open as his lungs fought to breathe. He was dead within seconds.

Sunny stood by the car, screaming, as she fumbled at her purse, yanking it open, digging blindly for her cell phone. She was too shocked to think straight. Too scared to see the danger she was in or the futility of her what she was doing. Her fingers finally closed around the phone. She pulled it out and immediately tried to dial.

The vagrant was upon her.

Sunny's mouth fell as she stared up at him. Quickly, she saw that this was no vagrant.

"Jesus Christ . . ." she muttered as the phone dropped from her hand.

He stared down at her.

Captain Howdy.

"Jesus Christ has *nothing* to do with this," he leered.

Then he swung a balled fist.

The punch caught her across the face like a sledgehammer. Her knees gave way, and she collapsed to the driveway.

The rain came down harder as though matching the ferocity with the violence Howdy brought upon his victims.

———

The sign at the edge of town stood proudly on the roadside, just as it always had:

Welcome to Helvertown, U.S.A.
A nice place to visit - A better place to live.

. . . Was what it should have said. Was what it did say a day before. The letters had since changed. The word *Helvertown* had been defaced, sprayed over crudely in black paint. The "VER" had been blotted out. And in its place, a second "L" had been sprayed roughly and the last word had also been changed.

It read:

Welcome to Hell Town, U.S.A.
A nice place to visit – A better place to *DIE.*

———

Over the next few days, the police station had turned into a veritable circus. Phones rang nonstop. Voices overlapped each other as citizens and reporters crammed into the lobby, hurling question after question at the overwhelmed desk sergeant. The air was fraught as tempers ran high. Reporters pressed forward, throwing tape recorders in every policeman's face they could find as if they personally deserved answers.

The entrance doors opened as Mike Gage and Steve Christian stormed in.

Mike had the look of someone about to snap, but Steve, he was already there. His clothes looked slept in. His face hung with large bags under his eyes. If he'd eaten in the past twelve hours, it didn't show. He was wired and burnt out.

Like blood to a shark, the reporters sensed them immediately, then swarmed, firing questions without waiting for any answers. The same questions were asked of every officer they met, but this time, the questions carried a more accusatory tone, as these were the two men in charge of the investigation.

Has Captain Howdy been apprehended?

Where are they?

What is the department doing to keep the public safe?

Gage—isn't it a conflict of interest, you being the lead detective?

Mike growled as he pushed his way through to the other side of the room. "No comment. No comment," he said dismissively.

Steve didn't hold back and was not as polite. He shouted over the gathered mass, turning to the uniformed officers stationed by the doors. "What the fuck are these assholes doing in here? I want them out. *Now.* Move them. Unless they have a report to file, they cannot be in here . . . And if they try to come back in, shoot them all!"

He didn't wait to see if the officer's heard him. He and Mike carried on, barreling a path across the crowd.

"Un-fuckin'-believable," Steve moaned under his breath.

"What do you expect?" Mike said, barely looking back. "Can't say I blame them."

They walked through the badge locked doors, leaving the public demands behind.

Mike continued. "Murders. Abductions . . . It's out of fucking control . . . And that latest one missing? Roth? You ever have any dealings with him?"

Steve sighed. It wasn't the first time he'd run into

that man. Jackson Roth had been at the receiving end of Steve's anger multiple times. "Real fucking sweetheart," he said. "I've busted him for pulling stunts at abortion clinics, beating his wife, creating a ruckus anywhere he could . . . He's a card-carrying NRA asshole, got local militia ties, real big on school prayer, and wants everything in one color, if you get my drift. God, guns, and Whites only."

Behind them, as they got farther into the bullpen, the sound of the lobby started to drift further away.

Mike turned as he got to his desk. "Fits real nice next to what we found in his basement."

"What was there?"

"Enough kiddie porn to keep him locked up for a damn long while."

Steve gave a bitter snort. "Another one for the Helvertown Hall of Fame." He shook his head. "This town, man . . . Shouldn't be surprised how many bad people are here, but I always am."

Mike couldn't disagree.

Steve continued. "What about the Macintoshes?"

"From the sounds of it, you could scratch out the name Jackson Roth and pencil in Sunny Macintosh," Mike said. "Delgado, Gagliardi, Savitch. They're all the same. Loud mouths with louder opinions, delusions of grandeur. Spiteful, hateful, asinine people. And utter pieces of shit. From what we can tell, they were all as awful as each other . . . And not surprisingly, all knew each other. Three of them had that kid stuff. As for Sunny and her husband? They were not into kids . . .

But . . ." He could not bring himself to complete the sentence.

"Oh, come on. What?"

Mike leaned on his desk, picked up a report, and handed it to Steve. "Check the second page."

Curiously, Steve took the manilla folder, opened it, and read. As he turned the first page, his eyes widened. He looked with a sickened expression at Mike. "You're fucking kidding me."

Mike smirked. "That Helvertown Hall of Fame is getting fuller by the minute."

Steve stopped, shaking his head. "And Hendricks is among them. You think a vigilante is picking off the towns trash? We got a witness that he was taken by a group of people and all these others gone . . . A new militia maybe?"

Mike didn't want to answer. Didn't want to admit that he could have stopped Carleton Hendricks from being abducted.

"Gage. Christian," Robbins called from a doorway on the other side of the room.

Beside the captain, red-faced and with cheeks streaked with tears, was Kelly Roth. The captain motioned to her as he continued. "Here's someone you need to talk to."

———

Consummate darkness, where, in the middle, a single candle was lit.

Hanging above, suspended upright in a bizarre, naked configuration of straps and steel, was Sunny Macintosh.

Her body was pulled in every direction. Arms stretched, legs spread, held in place by a thick harness that wrapped around her waist. Above her, a suspended ring of steel hung from the ceiling. This ring had dozens of holes along its edge, and placed in many of them were thin metal rods. Rods that had razor-sharp tips. They came down, point first and rested on various parts of her skin, gravity forcing their weight to pierce her. The ring above held the rods in place, and there was nothing Sunny could do to get away from it all. If she struggled in the harness, the rods would carve further into her. If she stayed still, she would have to endure the torment of dozens of metal rods cutting into her flesh.

She wanted to scream, but her mouth wouldn't open. It couldn't. Thick black stitches laced her lips shut, each one piercing and tying the skin together in a series of tight, methodical sutures.

A voice spoke through the blackness around her, theatrical and amused.

"Do you know the significance of the candles at these rites?" said Captain Howdy. "I always make sure that, at every lesson I teach, the only light is from flame. Nature's natural healer. The one insentient thing that destroys but also feeds itself. It is like a God we must all bow to in reverence." He approached Sunny, staring at her. "Now it's time to expand your spiritual horizons in the presence of this God. Trust me, you need this experience so you can ascend to a higher state of being."

Her eyes flicked toward him in panic. Her chest heaved, but each movement made the metal rods dig in a tiny bit farther.

His tattoos and piercings made him a terrifying figure to someone like Sunny. Someone saw these kinds of modifications as the devil's work. In her mind, Howdy was as bad as the devil, maybe in fact the devil incarnate, and for Howdy, he was happy to step into that role.

"What?" he asked, leaning closer. "You're already spiritually aware?"

Sunny looked at him fearfully and slowly nodded in confusion. Frantic sounds pushed out through her mouth threads. Muffled affirmations as she pleaded, not seeing the sarcasm in his question.

"Sunny, my dear old father always told me, 'Never confuse desperation with a spiritual awakening.'" He chuckled. "Well, he never actually *said* that . . . But I'm sure he would have meant it if he had the intellect."

He held up a handful of the same kind of rods that bore into her skin. Each with a wicked point at one end.

"It's time for the Kavadi Bearing," he said. "Embrace these, the spears of Shiva."

He placed one into a hole in the steel ring above her. The tip passed through, guided with care, until it came down into her bare breast.

He didn't drive it deep.

He left it resting on the skin.

The weight of it was just enough to pierce her.

Her body trembled violently in response to this added pain. The rod dug deeper with every shake as did the others that weighed down on her.

"Suffer my daughter to wear the Itiburi," he whispered with a tone of reverence. He brought his face close to hers. "Will the daughter accept the Itiburi?"

Sunny tried to keep still, but the new spike in her brought a fresh wave of pain with it, which made her body spasm in an animalistic panic.

Her gagged screams pushed through the seams in her lips.

"I'll take that as a 'yes,'" he said, amused. "But please try not to move. You don't want to hurt yourself."

He took the rest of the rods in his hand and, one by one, inserted them through the steel ring. Each slid down through their hole. Each found a new part of her flesh. Each drew a new wave of agony upon her. Her screams were desperate and wild, though contained behind the thread in her lips.

Around, in the shadows, others watched. Others bound and gagged in different ways. Some hanging. Some standing. Gene Gagliardi. Jackson Roth. Mary Delgado. Rainer Savitch. Each one of their mouths had been sewn shut like hers. Their eyes were wide as they stared in terror at what was happening to her.

Captain Howdy continued.

"This pain is an important part of our bonding experience," he said to Sunny. "A physical horror that binds us even closer. The very intensity of this experience helps to widen the gulf between us"—he paused, nodding toward the other captives—"and those who have not shared it yet."

More rods slid into place. More spikes broke into her.

As Sunny jerked, she cried and screamed behind her bound mouth. And as she did, the thread pulled at her lips tore at the skin, blood seeping from the fresh wounds.

"You must transcend what your body translates as pain," he said, enjoying this far too much. "Turn it into pleasure. Then into a spiritual event. *You* do not feel the pain. The *body* feels the pain. And pain is just an impulse sent through your nerves. You can tell your mind to process the information differently. That is a power we *all* have."

She struggled harder. The rods felt as if they were burning, burrowing into her muscle, as her mouth strained to open. The stitches began to tear more. Slowly, her lips started splitting along the seams. The threads were not going to give way, as they were too strong. Her lips, though, were soft and weak and ripped all at once, spewing blood down her chin and onto the floor.

It was a single final shriek of agony that split the darkness of the room.

A shriek that was the last noise Sunny Macintosh would make.

As the pain took total control of her, she convulsed

in a panic trying to get away, and slowly, the spiked rods drove in. Much farther in.

Then silence.

Her body went limp.

The rods jutted from her front and back like porcupine spines.

Her torn, bloodied mouth hung open.

Captain Howdy looked at her. Unfazed. "Or maybe you are too unevolved, and the pain got to be much. Pity."

———

"What the fuck do you mean you knew?" Steve shouted, standing in front of Mike who was sitting at his desk.

"Please, keep it down," Mike whispered, eying the room to make sure no one heard.

"Oh, bullshit, Mike. Were you even gonna tell me if Roth's daughter hadn't come in?"

"What difference would it have made?"

Steve exhaled and had to restrain himself. "There I was, putting out the theory that it was a new vigilante militia cleaning up the town by taking the towns assholes, when you fucking *knew* it was the assholes who were the ones doing the taking? And they took Hendricks. Another asshole."

Mike couldn't take the guilt now that everything was in the open. "I could have stopped it, okay? I could have got out my car and scared them off."

"And you didn't because?"

"Because I wanted him *gone!*"

Steve couldn't blame his partner, but he was hurt that Mike kept it from him.

Mike sighed. "I'm sorry, okay?"

Steve grabbed his own chair and brought it over to the desk. "Hey, I get it. But you gotta keep me in the loop. We gotta find them. And if it's a kidnapping gone wrong or they're all holed up taking turns in battering Hendricks, then we gotta find out where, when, and how, okay?"

Mike nodded, ashamed.

Steve changed tacks. "Where's Toni and Gen?"

"Toni's with her mom," he said. "Gen's away at college. I just don't—"

The laptop next to him let out a sharp chime.

Both men turned to the screen.

A new instant message had appeared:

CaptHowdy579: *The dead are so dreadfully dead, when they're very dead.*

"Fucking hell," Steve said. "He's online?"

Mike's could not hide his surprise. "Maybe it's like the scene of a crime. They always come back to it . . . We gotta make sure it's actually him and not a kid pissin' around."

He placed his fingers to the keyboard and typed:

MGage275: *Identify yourself.*

He hit Return.

A pause.

Another chime.

CaptHowdy579: *You like your shiny badge, don't you, Michael?*

"Tell him yes," Steve said. "But you'd prefer it if it was sticking out of his fucking lower intestine."

Mike ignored the threat. He typed again, this time speaking the words aloud as he did.

"Do any of your hostages need medical attention?"

Return.

Before any response could come, the desk phone rang, making both of them jump. Steve grabbed it.

"12th precinct, Detective Christian speaking."

There was a pause.

Then his expression fell. He slowly held the phone out toward Mike.

From the other end of the line came the unmistakable voice of Captain Howdy.

"Why stay online?" he said.

Holy fuck, Steve mouthed.

Mike took the phone cautiously. He brought it to his ear.

Howdy continued. "I'm one of those who consider the superfluous essential," the voice said. "And you are quite superfluous."

"Are you ready to come in?" he asked carefully.

"You think your badge is power," Howdy's voice replied confidently. "It's not. Knowledge is power. Your badge isn't even permanent."

Steve, without a word, picked up another phone and started dialing fast.

On Mike's call, the voice kept coming.

"My badges, however," Howdy said, "I can never take off. They set me apart from all others until the day I die. My badges are forever. Yours is a mere convenience."

"My badge represents the law," he said. "Your badges mean nothing to anyone except you."

Steve whispered into the second phone. "I need a trace on Detective Gage's outside line. Now."

"Which law is that, Michael?" Howdy asked. "The law that found me not guilty or the law that allowed others to take matters into their own hands and make this what it is? For that was not me. As well you know. So, I cannot be held to blame to what came next. I am the wronged, protecting myself."

"I can assure you they will not get away with any of it," Mike said. "They were wrong,"

"No. YOU were wrong," Howdy snapped, on the border of losing his temper. "You let it happen. I saw you." His tone then changed, becoming lighter. "But that was then, this is now. And now, I've discovered a whole new flock in need of spiritual awakening through my hand."

Steve shot Mike a look, a signal. Keep him talking.

"Can I ask where you are, or would that be a useless thing to ask?" Mike said as calmly as he could.

Without warning, the line went dead. A harsh tone blared into Mike's ear.

"Dammit," he said as he lowered the receiver.

Steve was not so reserved. He slammed his phone down so hard it bounced off the desk. "*Fuck!*"

His frustration echoed through the otherwise quiet bullpen.

———

Captain Howdy sat perfectly cross-legged on the floor of the dark torture room, among the collection of shadowed bodies that lined the walls. With a laptop in front of him, his latex gloves were covered in dried blood as his fingers typed. The screen had lines of code, patterns, messages, all parts of his plan. But then one thing flashed up, a news article about the closing of Xibalba. He read it with interest.

A moan next to him pulled his attention away from the screen. He didn't need to turn to know what it was. As he spoke, his voice sounded kind, as if he were speaking to a lover. "Some people want everything given to them with a big red bow," he said. "But not you . . ." He turned, putting the laptop down and rising from the floor. "*You* don't want a thing."

Across from him, barely visible in the dull light, Jackson Roth's body was cradled in a bizarre wooden rig. A cage-like structure built from long, crisscrossed poles, lashed together and bolted with thick eye-hooks. He lay face down. His limbs hung limply through the spaces between the beams. He was barely holding onto any semblance of consciousness.

Howdy stepped closer as he crouched beside his prisoner, grabbed a fistful of his hair, and pulled his head up.

"*Do* you want anything?" he asked, accusing.

Roth didn't answer. He couldn't. Not anymore. He could only tremble with the pain.

The sutures across his mouth were more than others were given. The stitches were tiger and thicker. And they were not alone. New ones had been added to his face. Thin threads also stitched his eyelids tightly shut. His cheeks were caked in fresh—as well as old—blood that seeped out from the wounds.

Howdy stared, admiring the work. It was dark in here, but his eyes had adjusted so much that he could see as well as if there had been a light on.

"How much is enough, do you think?" he asked Jackson in a whisper. "It's been said that the road to excess leads to the palace of wisdom, for we never know what is enough until we know what is *more* than enough."

Reaching to one side, he grabbed a small tackle box that sat beside the rig. He opened it and removed a gleaming fishhook. A large barbed twisting of metal that was sharp enough to split leather. He took it in one hand and pressed the point to a thick piece of Jackson's back, teasingly stroking it across his skin, then, without warning, drove it through with a rage-soaked grunt.

Roth bucked violently, forced back into full consciousness.

He tried to scream. He tried to escape. But it was futile.

"Oh, stop being a baby," Howdy cackled.

He then grabbed a thick cord and attached to the freshly embedded hook. With a steady hand, he ran the line up to the wooden rig above. He pulled slowly, and as he did, Jackson's skin stretched up grotesquely, pulling at his body.

Roth writhed, his cries louder, each motion making his suffering worse.

Captain Howdy didn't even glance down as he took another large hook from the tackle box. "You don't like me very much, do you, Jackson?" he asked.

This second hook was bigger, crueler in its shape. He pressed it onto another piece of Jackson's back, then thrust it in. Hooking it through. Another anchor for the suspension that was to come.

"I understand," Howdy continued casually. "In our society, physical difference frightens people, sometimes turns them on. Which frightens them so much more."

He guided a cord through the second hook up to the frame above.

Another yank. The skin stretched up. Another part of Jackson's body lifted off the wooden rig, hanging by flesh and cord.

"You can be as deviant as hell inside . . ." He yanked

harder, tightening the cord's hold. "But do one little physical thing, like, oh, I don't know, tattoo your face . . . and, man, people freak out."

The next hook was grabbed and then went in. Jackson's body jerked yet again. Helpless. Gagged. Blind.

"It's a curse of our society that we have to fit into a rigid pattern in order to belong," Howdy continued. "There's no room for imagination. No room for creativity."

Another hook. Another stab. Another chord. Another yank upward.

Jackson was sobbing. The tears fought to break free of the stitching.

Howdy raised his eyebrows and leaned in, feigning surprise. "Are you actually crying?"

He crouched and got closer. Right up to Jackson's face. Their noses almost touching. He watched as the tears squeezed out from behind the stitched lids and ran down the sides of Jackson's cheeks, bringing blood out with them.

"Hey," he whispered, "there's no crying in spiritual awakenings. You're not a child . . . Your childhood was over the moment you knew you were going to die . . . You should be quiet in abject awe. Tears in the face of ascension weakens its impact."

CHAPTER 10

REVENGE

A car rolled down the stretch of empty freeway. Not yet night and not still day, the dusk was painting everything orange.

Mike stared ahead, answering a call on his mobile phone as Steve drove, one hand on the wheel, the other resting against the gear shift.

"Hey," Toni said. "This a bad time?"

Mike rubbed the corner of his temple with his free hand. "No, it's fine," he sighed. "Just dropped a witness off . . . How's your mom's?"

"Fine . . ." She quickly changed the subject. "Is Gen okay?"

Mike furrowed his brow. "What are you talking about? She's at college."

"No, I called. Her roommate said she left yesterday."

Mike's eyes widened.

"They said *you* called to pick her up . . . Mike, what's going on?"

He didn't reply. He stared ahead as his world fell out beneath him.

"Mike?" Her voice rippled with fear. "Where is she?"

Mike looked in panic at Steve.

"My house. *Now.*"

Steve didn't ask any questions. He had overheard enough. He punched his foot on the gas pedal. The tires squealed as the car shot forward, cutting across the lanes.

———

Farther in the city, a major intersection, layered with painted crosswalks, traffic lights, and four long lanes crisscrossing each other, had a rush hour congestion at gridlock. Cars progressed at a snail's paces as their horns honked with futile annoyance.

Then came the screech.

Rubber cried out.

A car burst through the painted lines into the heart of the intersection, weaving past bumpers and careening around the queue. Cutting through with desperation.

Toni Gage was sitting behind the wheel.

Her hands were gripped on the steering wheel. Her face radiated one thing: panic.

In one hand, she dialed her phone as she shot around the traffic and brought it to her ear. Just as the last two dozen times. There was nothing. A fast busy signal that spat back at her.

"Please, God, no, no, no!" she cried. "Don't let this be happening."

Another turn. A hard right. The tires screamed again as the car jumped across lanes, barely missing a cluster of pedestrians as she shot past the still traffic, metal only inches from metal.

More horns, this time at her, joined in with the screams from drivers she nearly hit.

But she didn't slow down.

She dialed again. Another busy tone.

She looked at the phone, then at the road. Or what was the road?

"Oh, shit!"

The path ahead was suddenly missing. In its place, a construction site had chewed up two lanes. Trucks, equipment, barricades, and a handful of orange-vested workers created a wall of obstruction.

The oncoming paths around it were gridlocked, with no other way for her to go.

She gripped the wheel, swerved hard, and drove up onto the sidewalk. Her foot hit the gas. Pedestrians screamed as they threw themselves out of the way, diving for cover.

The car tore past the construction site, then veered hard left and bounced back onto the road, speeding away like a rocket.

———

"*Gen!*" Mike shouted.

Arriving at his house, the front door lock would not work. He slammed himself into the door, trying to force it open. But it wouldn't budge. He pressed harder, shoulder first. There was something behind the door. Blocking it.

Throwing his weight over and over, eventually, the door had no choice but to relent but only a fraction. He managed to wedge it open enough to squeeze through, his side brushing past a pair of scattered bags jammed under the door, Genevieve's bags. The hallway was a mess, and the side table had been cracked in two. The vase smashed on the floor. The coat rack ripped from the wall.

He cursed himself. If he hadn't spent the previous night at the station, sleeping at his desk, he would have been home for whatever happened.

His gun was drawn.

"*Genevieve!*" he called out.

Steve entered from behind. He saw the mess, the disarray. "Oh, fuck no!" he couldn't help but say. He moved the bags out of the way, letting the door swing open fully.

Mike didn't wait. His gun was cocked, and he took off, moving from room to room, clearing each space in rapid order.

"Check upstairs!" he called back to his partner.

Steve nodded, pulling his weapon. "Gen?" he called out as he took two steps at a time.

Downstairs, Mike finished his sweep of the rooms.

He didn't need to check upstairs. He already knew the answer before he heard Steve call down.

"CLEAR!" came the expected confirmation.

Outside, a car could be heard skidding to a stop on the street. Within seconds, Toni was there, standing in the doorway, frantic.

She rushed in, out of breath, still clutching her keys.

She looked around, calling out. "Gen? Oh, please, honey, where are you?! Genevieve!"

Mike stepped out from the living room, fighting his anger and tears back in equal measure. "She's gone."

Toni walked over fast, the panic burning in her eyes.

"Gone?! What do you mean?" She looked past him. "What the fuck is—"

Her words stopped as she saw it. Something Mike had overlooked. He was too busy looking for people, not objects. He had not noticed the open laptop through the doorway, resting on the dining room table. The laptop that had been switched on.

Steve came down and saw Mike and Toni both staring into the room beside them. He followed their gaze.

On the table, the laptop's screen was dark. A small black webcam had been mounted to the top, and it stared back at them like an eye, its red light on . . . They were being watched.

And on cue, as he waited for them, the screen suddenly changed. It was not turned off but a video feed that had been covered. And here, now that there was an audience, was the reveal.

There, on screen staring at them, was Captain Howdy. Live.

He stared through the lens, his face a perverse mix of glee and malice. "What, no hello for your favorite guy?" he asked with a laugh.

Mike moved to the chair in front of the computer and sat down, staring at the screen. "Where is she?" he asked through gritted teeth.

Captain Howdy tilted his head to one side, regarding Mike's suppressed rage. "Do you mean the lovely Genevieve? Oh, she's with me. I'm taking *especially* good care of her." He turned his gaze sideways, directly at Steve, who was looking angrier by the second.

"You gotta love this technology," Howdy said. "Look, you even brought Detective what's-his-name, falling apart at the seams, I see. You need to breathe, sir. You look like you're about to pop . . . You'll have an aneurysm."

Toni pushed by and leaned closer to the screen, needing to see, needing to confront.

Howdy grinned wider as he saw her.

"Is that the lovely Mrs. Gage? What an expected yet pleasant surprise. I am pleased to meet your acquaintance, albeit in this digital space. My name is Captain Howdy. But you can call me Sir."

Toni's could not stop screaming her words. "What have you done with my daughter, you bastard?!"

"Toni!" Mike snapped. Knowing that screaming could not do any good.

But it was too late.

"Ooh, fiery," Howdy said. "I need that. Maybe I took the wrong one after all?"

"Let me talk to him," Mike said quietly to his wife. "I—"

"Why?!" Toni shouted at the screen. "Why Genevieve?! What did she do to you?!"

Captain Howdy looked satisfied. "She didn't do a thing," he said. "Not her . . . Oh, I get it . . . You didn't tell her, Michael, did you? That you did this? That none of this would be happening if you stopped them from taking me."

Mike didn't answer.

"You didn't, did you?" Howdy's voice then sounded almost soothing. "How human of you."

Toni turned to her husband. "Tell me what? What's he talking about? What did you do?"

Mike said nothing. He just stared at the screen.

Steve, meanwhile, had stepped back, out of range of the camera, and was whispering quietly into his phone. He walked around the table and caught Mike's attention. *They're on it*, he mouthed, motioning to the phone. *Keep him online*. Not that either of them thought it would do any good. Howdy never stayed on the line long enough to be traced, but in Steve's mind, it was worth a shot.

Howdy smiled at something off-screen. "You know," he said, "pain is a uniquely personal experience. The most personal experience there is aside from death."

He turned back to the lens, back to his captive

audience. "Hey, kids, don't try this at home." He beamed.

The image on screen turned.

A tight shot, an extreme close-up, shaky, with a digital lag.

It was a woman's breast.

Ten hypodermic needles had been pushed through the flesh, aligned in a slow arc across the skin.

Within seconds, Howdy's latex-gloved hands came into shot and inserted another. The body jerked in response.

"Short is the ornament, long is the pain," Howdy said, amused.

The camera soon moved again, upward, slow and deliberate.

The face came into frame.

The face that broke Mike and Toni.

Genevieve.

Her mouth had been sewn shut once more. The needle having pierced the scar tissue from her last torment.

And she could see them back. She could see her parents. Helplessly watching her torture. She tried to speak, but the only sounds she could make were moans. Her eyes stared, pleading.

"No," Toni sobbed. "Oh God! Oh God! *No!*"

Mike clenched his fists. His rage finally breaking. Unable to keep his detective's composure anymore. He was no longer a cop. He was her father.

"You . . ." He shouted, trying to find the words. "I'll—"

Steve couldn't see the screen, so he walked back around the table. He gasped in horror as he saw Genevieve.

Toni exploded in tears and fury. "You sadistic sack of shit, I'll kill you! So help me God I will kill you!"

"Toni!" Mike called out, tears streaming down his cheeks as well. "*Stop!*"

He jumped out of the chair, grabbed her by the shoulders, and pulled her back out of the room, away from the webcam's glare. She fought him at first, but he moved in close and whispered with intensity.

"This animal has Gen! Do you really want to set him off more?"

Captain Howdy's voice floated to them from the laptop's speakers. "I'm interested in heightening people's awareness. Altering states through primitive rituals. She is ascending so well." He peered into the lens, seeing from his screen that no one was in front of the camera anymore.

"Hey, where did everyone go?"

Mike held Toni in the hallway, her lips trembling, eyes full of fire and helpless fury. But she didn't scream again. She knew Mike was right. He kissed her on the cheek and turned back.

Returning to the screen, he sat in his chair and leaned in close.

Out of the view of the webcam, Steve, meanwhile,

was still on the phone, as he could not stop looking at Genevieve in agony.

"It's going to be okay, honey," Mike said. "I'm going to find you. Just hang in there. I'll be there soon."

"Ooh," Howdy purred. "Scary . . . May I ask *when* will you get here? And how do you even know where here is?"

"How about this . . . How about you take me instead?" Mike offered. "Me for her . . . Let my daughter go."

Captain Howdy paused as if weighing the offer. "Hmmm? Tempting. But you see, Gen and I have only . . . brushed the surface of . . . our relationship. I've invested a lot of time and energy into her now." He moved closer to the camera. On the screen, his lips and sharp teeth filled the entire frame. "So much flesh . . . so little time . . . Then again . . . you look like you will be a lot of fun . . . Leave it with me."

The feed then cut off. The screen went black.

Mike turned to Steve, desperate for an answer.

Steve shook his head as he lowered his phone. "No," he said quietly. "Like last time. Fucker cuts off right before we can get a lock."

The sound of plastic and metal hitting wood as Mike grabbed the laptop and smashed it in a fury onto the edge of the dining room table. Pieces broke. Sparks jumped from the machine as he roared in anger.

Then, with all his effort, he shut his eyes and dropped the laptop onto the floor. Calming himself. *Needing* to calm himself. *Needing* to focus.

"Toni," he suddenly called out as he got out of the chair and ran out of the room.

————

The door gave after three kicks. Metal creaked, then groaned, then surrendered with a brittle crack as it swung open.

Officer Scott entered first, late forties, flashlight sweeping the room. Behind him was Officer Jarmel. His gun raised as he tried not to breathe too loudly. The stink inside had hit them both at once. A stench of decay, filth, and the sharp acid of human excretion.

"Unit 6," Scott said into his radio. "At the possible B&E . . . The lock's been jimmied. We're inside now."

Static clicked, then the dispatcher's voice came back.

"Unit 6, advance for the possible trespass. Over."

Scott raised his flashlight, moving deeper into the room.

"Wait . . ." he said, seeing something. "What's that up there?"

He stopped.

"What the?"

His beam froze on something. Flesh. Raw and pale, pierced by steel fishhooks. A line ran from the hook, tugging the skin upward, taut and grotesque. He moved his beam to the left.

Another hook. Then another. Six inches apart. Each one driven deep into skin and meat, pulling at a body.

"Jesus Christ . . ." Scott whispered.

Behind them, Jarmel turned on the light switch.

The room came to life in one sickening instant.

It was a body. Suspended by fishhooks, naked and stretched inside a wooden cradle built from long beams and steel braces. A lattice of meat and metal.

It was Jackson Roth.

His body was riddled with metal. At least fifty, maybe more hooks, had sunken deep into his back, chest, legs, arms, shoulders, even his neck. Each hook was then connected to a cord, each cord threaded through a separate eye-hook in the surrounding frame. He was not just suspended upward, but his skin was also stretched out in every direction of the wooden frame. He was pulled in a star pattern so tight it barely held. His mouth and eyes stitched closed.

He wasn't dead but was barely alive.

Scott stared as he realized that he wasn't the only victim here. "Oh, Mother of God."

The rest of the room was bright.

This was a torture chamber.

Victims lined the walls, each caught in some new level of horror.

Sunny Macintosh was still in her Kavadi Bearing harness. There were more rods now. Dozens. Her torso looked like an iron maiden had closed around her without piercing straight through.

Rainer Savitch was crucified upside down against the back wall. His eyes were open yet hollow. Bored out and dangling from the sockets on his cheeks. Alive and moaning.

Mary Delgado was draped in lead fishing weights, each one hooked into her skin like bait on a line.

Gene Gagliardi hung from the ceiling, upside down, suspended by two massive meat hooks driven through his heels.

And Genevieve . . .

She was there, a human pincushion. Her body peppered with hundreds of small needles and pins in symmetrical rows. Her head tilted down, neck too weak to lift anymore.

Then something moved from behind her.

Jarmel turned too late.

A flash of metal cut across the young officer's throat. His voice didn't even rise. Blood spilled over his uniform as he dropped, gurgling, eyes wide.

Scott didn't see it in time and only caught a glimpse before a face came grinning back at him, lit by the bright overhead lights.

"Boo!" Captain Howdy said playfully, before darting into the dark hallway beyond this room.

Scott's hand shook as he raised his radio.

"This is Unit 6 . . ." His voice cracked. "Ten-thirteen . . . Unit 6 . . . ten-thirteen . . . Officer down . . ." He hesitated, the next word coming out in a whimper. "Please . . . Someone, help us."

Within ten few minutes, flashing lights bounced off the brick exterior of Captain Howdy's lair. Police cruisers and ambulances jammed the perimeter. Medics pushed stretchers toward the waiting vehicles. Screams cut through the buzz of chatter. Some were cries of relief. Some weren't.

Victims were wheeled out on gurneys, shaking, half-conscious, stitched and bleeding.

The press had also caught wind of what happened and surged on the scene like a wave, barely held back by makeshift cordon of tape and officers. Around them, camera bulbs flashed. Boom mics stretched forward, desperate for a soundbite.

Inside, the torture room had emptied of victims. They had been taken away, but the remnants of their pain was still here, lingering on every surface. In every pool of blood. In every pile of filth. In every discarded pin, needle, and wire.

Captain Robbins was on one side, supervising the cataloguing of evidence as Mike and Steve were looking around the room.

Mike's eyes were fixed in front of him. Staring without blinking. A thousand-yard stare.

"This can't be an accident. He wanted them to be found," he said.

Steve was fighting the urge to throw up. "You think he's the one that called it in?"

Mike didn't answer, but that's exactly what he thought.

He stood in front of a table in the corner. Among

the scattered tools and old candles sat the laptop, still open, humming.

On the keyboard sat a single matchbook. Curiously, he picked it up, then turned it over. It was plain black, aside from a red X on the front. An X Michael was familiar with.

He opened the matchbook up, and there it was. A message had been written in careful print:

MICHAEL,
"HE WHO RESEMBLES THE DEAD IS
MOST RELUCTANT TO DIE."
C.H.

Mike quickly pocketed the matchbook without anyone noticing.

"So, if he called this all in . . ." Steve said as he looked around the room. "Why? We may never have found this house, at least not now."

"It's all a game to him," Mike replied. "He's getting off on fucking with us. He wanted us to come here. Wanted us to find them. Wanted . . . To taunt us."

Inside the ambulance, Genevieve lay wrapped in shock blankets, her skin pale. The stitches on her mouth removed. Her skin covered in bandages and plasters. An paramedic knelt beside her, checking her vitals, monitoring her pupils, being extremely gentle.

Next to her, Toni held her hand tightly.

Walking out from the house, Mike approached. "Is she alright?" he asked the paramedic.

"Nothing life-threatening that I can see . . . So, yeah . . . physically, at least, she's okay. Can't say anything about the mental effects, though." It didn't matter that Genevieve could here, she was in no state to understand. She was just staring up at the roof of the ambulance. Lost in her terror.

Toni leaned down and kissed her forehead. She spoke to her daughter as if she could hear and answer. "Honey . . . I need to talk to your father outside for a second, okay?"

Genevieve just stared blankly as Toni let go of her hand and stepped out of the vehicle, then dragged her husband to one side.

Without warning, she shoved Mike hard against the side of a parked police cruiser.

"*Kill him*," she hissed. "You find him, and you kill him. *Right now*." She moved in closer, jabbing a finger at his chest. "You've done it by the book long enough, and it didn't fucking work . . . We've got Genevieve back *again*. Now there's no fucking excuse. No more bullshit. Put that animal down!"

"Toni," Mike began before she cut him off.

"Find him. Hurt him. Kill him."

Mike looked ashamed. "I . . . I can't," he replied.

Toni stepped back, staring at him like he was disgusting.

"Can't—or won't?" she asked, before turning and walking back over to the ambulance.

Mike remembered the matchbook. The one with the message. The one with red X on. The red X that was the same as on the sign on that club.

———

Xibalba had been shut down for years. After Carleton Hendricks had been apprehended, the city immediately revoked the club's license, fearing that it was a hotbed of crime full of others wanting to torture 'normal' citizens. The citizens' voices were heard.

The sign was gone. The building left derelict.

Inside, the dance floor once nave was now a shell of what it once was. Drop cloths draped each piece of furniture, making them look like ghosts. Dust and filth clung to everything. The air was stagnant, untouched, having been locked inside. The bar sat half drunk, still with undrunk bottles, left without care as the doors locked for good. Where there was once music, movement and primal elation, was now just a hollow void. An echo.

But when Mike got there. The doors were no longer locked. They had been left wide open. Expectant.

He walked in and locked the doors behind him. Trapping himself inside with whatever was waiting. Making sure there was no clear escape.

He had made his excuses at the lair and left the investigation on scene, claiming a need to be with his family, but he was no actor. He could not fool everyone. As down the street, a car soon pulled up, having followed Mike here. Detective Christian. He had kept his distance trailing and was sitting outside, having watched Mike cross the road and enter the club.

"Hendricks?" Mike called out. His voice echoed around the room.

With his gun out, he walked around, checking each corner.

Mike knew he should call for backup. He knew this was a trap. But he had to do it alone. He had to face this monster and bring him in. He had to be the one to beat him. For what he had done to everyone, to his daughter—twice. He had a score to settle, mainly to himself, and it would be done his way. He could not stop until Carleton Hendricks was locked up for good. Rotting in a cell.

He tried to gather all his bravery, all his training. He could not let the monster win.

"Hendricks?" he called out again as he stepped onto the dark dance floor.

A reply then came back.

"Hendricks?" Howdy said from somewhere in the dark. "That poor bastard died when you let me get lynched . . . You can call me Howdy or Captain."

Mike couldn't see where the voice came from. "For a man who's gone to such great lengths to modify his appearance, you're damn reluctant to be seen," he said. "Where the fuck are you, Carleton?"

The voice responded, sounding annoyed. "You insist on calling me that to what? Anger me? Well, it's working . . . A name isn't a matter for indifference. It implies a whole series of relationships between the one who bears it and the source from where it is derived. So, I ask again, call me Captain Howdy."

"From where it's derived?" Mike said, gripping his gun tighter, trying to see through the darkness. "Your father was a war hero, a marine, Captain Bradford Hendricks. And this . . . This is how you honor his name, by taking a dumb name from a horror film?"

The irritation cracked through. "*Call me Captain Howdy.*"

"Whatever, Carleton . . . Get out here!"

The voice grunted. "You need to talk . . . then talk. I gave you everything you asked for. You offered yourself . . . So, now succumb to me, Detective!"

"Why can't you show yourself?" Mike asked. "Maybe you're not used to dealing with anyone who's not restrained and whose mouth isn't sewn shut. Is that what's bothering you, Carleton? That I have a voice."

A pause lingered.

The anger was almost manifest each time Mike said his real name. But Howdy pushed it all aside as he spoke. "Some regard it as evidence of bravery for a man to go into battle carrying no weapon that can do any harm at a distance. It's easy to be hard from behind your momma's skirt, do you agree? Yet we had a deal. Your life for hers. I gave her back, but now you fight me like a coward?"

Mike didn't move. He understood. "You mean the gun? Here." He threw it to the floor. Not the sanest thing he had ever done but something he did on instinct more than training. "You know, it's hilarious," he continued, stepping forward, trying to see more in the surrounding shadows, "that for all your lectures and endless preening, you're really just another prick with a persecution complex. You pick on those weaker . . . then run off and hide like a coward. I've seen it over and over a thousand times."

Then a soft, bitter voice came from behind him.

"Michael . . ."

He turned, then saw him. Twenty feet away, emerging from the darkness, was Captain Howdy. Naked, terrifying.

"How about I come over there and beat you?" Howdy asked. "That is what you understand, isn't it? Violence without cause? It's all you seem to care about. At least the violence I offered has a higher purpose. Yours is just stupidity masked in caveman ethics."

Mike didn't flinch, nor was he intimidated. "Sure, come on, then. Let's be cavemen. What's stopping you? You're bigger than me. You can't be worried that I'd win, right?"

With a smirk, Howdy strode across the dance floor, and as he did, Mike didn't wait. He charged fast.

He swung first, wide and heavy, aimed at Howdy's head.

But Howdy was quicker and much, much stronger.

He caught Mikes's arm midair with a single iron-like grip. He pulled it out, leaving Mike's body wide open for attack. Vulnerable.

Howdy smiled. Then struck.

Two hard knees drove into Mike's midsection. Each one landing like a shotgun blast.

Mike doubled over, gasping, unable to brace himself.

"First you dream, then you die," Howdy laughed.

The third knee came hard and high, straight to Mike's face.

Outside, Steve had reached the club's locked doors.

He tried the handles. They didn't budge.

"*Gage!*" he shouted in panic.

Inside, Mike's body crashed onto one of the nearby tables. The impact knocked the air out of him. He barely had time to inhale before Howdy was on top of him, fists already flying in blurring barrage.

The attack came fast and brutally. Without hesitation. Without mercy. And without an ounce of rage. Howdy's face was calm and almost zen-like. Nothing he was doing was an exertion or fueled with emotion. It was just what was happening. What Mike had asked for and what Howdy gave him dissociated from all emotion. And Mike couldn't respond. Couldn't get up. Couldn't block. He was caught in the middle of a storm. His training had taught him how to subdue a violent subject, but this was beyond violence. Beyond any normality.

Howdy smiled as he brought another blow down, this one timed to a melody in his head that he now sang aloud.

"*Everywhere, there's lots of piggies . . .*" he sang.

A kick to the ribs as if choreographed.

"*Living piggy lives.*"

Another punch, square to the face.

"*You can see them out to dinner with their piggy wives . . .*"

Mike barely held on. Blood poured from his split lip. One eye was already swelling shut as his bruised cheek screamed at him in agony.

Howdy leaned in. His breath was warm as he smiled. "*Clutching forks and knives . . .*"

His hands then wrapped around Mike's throat as his fingers tightened.

"*To kill their bacon.*"

Mike's eyes fluttered, gasping.

Then everything went dark.

The building was a fortress. Steve ran from the locked door to every boarded-up window on every side, to every possible entrance there could be. But nothing was accessible. All possible access had been sealed off.

Then the music inside started.

A thick pounding drifted through the brickwork toward him.

Something then sounded above it all. Louder than the music. A terrified and angry cry.

Steve had to move faster. He dropped to one knee at a rear window and began tearing at the boards with both hands. Using all of his strength in an attempt to tear his way inside.

A few moments before, Mike's world had flooded back in pieces.

He managed to open his eyes as the high ceiling above blurred in a smearing of colored lights and shadow. He was lying on a table in the middle of the dance floor, broken and beaten as the lights rotated wildly around the room along to the music that played through the speakers.

Then came the other sounds. Mechanical, ratcheting sounds.

Above him, coming into his hazy view, two meat hooks came down. Each were attached to long lengths of chains that fed up into wheels, then zigzagged across the ceiling and down to a large winch that controlled them. It clacked loudly as it unspooled the chain.

The hook's points glinted in the multicolored lights as the clacking came to a sudden stop, leaving them inches above Mike's chest.

Then, from behind, Howdy's arm shot out and

looped around Mike's neck, yanking him upright to a seating position.

"Not fighting back? Huh?" Howdy said. "Are you beaten already? 'Tis very disappointing."

With a free hand, he reached forward and ripped open Mike's shirt. He grabbed one of the meat hooks that hung close and aimed the point toward Mike's chest.

"You know," Howdy laughed. "Your sweet Genevieve took so long to give up. She fought. Clawed. Screamed. Pleaded. It was quite wonderful. I guess she takes after her mother. Maybe I should find her and see?"

Mike could only let out an anguished cry.

Steve had heard it. The full-throated agony as he clawed at the boarded window.

Nails splintered as the wood cracked.

Something broke loose inside Mike. He thought his fight was gone. That it was over. But the adrenaline surged through him in a second wind. His hand shot back, clawed for anything and found Howdy's face.

His hand closed around the steel bullring through his nose and, with one sharp tug, tore it out. Ripping through the septum. But that was not all. As Howdy screamed, Mike's hand reached down, grabbed what he could, and yanked.

. . .

In one pull, he tore out Howdy's Ampallang bar. Splitting through his gland, ripping it in half.

Howdy did not see either attack coming, and he howled in pain as he staggered backward. Blood spilled down his face and thighs.

Mike scrambled off the table, coughing and dragging himself across the dance floor. He turned back just in time to see Howdy, wild-eyed and frothing, running toward him again but smiling. Twisting the immense agony he was in into some awful pleasure.

Mike looked for anything he could and threw it forward. A candle on a table. An dusty glass. A chair. All was useless against the bloody man getting closer.

Howdy slowed to a stride as Mike was backed up against a wall, with nowhere to go. "Don't be afraid to die," he said with a wavering voice. "Death is the standard by which the reality and depth of all activities can be judged . . . And I make this promise. Your wife and Genevieve will be joining you real soon. I'll make sure to take my time with her, though. That is the price for what you just did. I was going to let them go after . . . But you had to try and teach the teacher. Which is never tolerated."

He lunged, grabbing Mike by the collar and dragging him back toward the dangling chains. Mike tried to fight Howdy, but he moved Mike like a doll. Getting to the table, Howdy wrapped one of the chains around Mike's neck and pulled hard on it, turning him to stare into his eyes.

"I will take you to the brink of death, then pull you back. Then take you there again."

With his last bit of effort, he used it all as he pulled his legs up tight, leaped into the air, and launched a double kick straight into Howdy's midsection.

The impact knocked Howdy backward, releasing the chain from around Mike's neck.

And Mike didn't wait. He screamed, grabbing one of the meat hooks, and ran forward, dragging the chain behind him. Before Howdy could get to his feet, the metal hook met with flesh. Driven through his shoulder. Past skin, muscle and bone and out the other side.

The agony was more than Howdy had ever experienced. It was something he had not expected. A pain that he could not subdue immediately. Even his split Ampallang piercing was easy to enjoy. This, though . . . He shrieked as his nerves seared.

"Short is the pain," Mike yelled through clenched teeth, "long is the ornament." He turned, staggered across the room to the mechanical winch, and slammed on its red button.

The clanking sounded loudly as the mechanism kicked into gear and started to wind the chain inward.

Trying to pull against it, Howdy could not stop the hook pulling him across the room, dragging him by his shoulder. It had been jammed beneath the joint, so there was no escape as then wrenched him upward. His legs dangled and kicked, powerless against it. The pain from his groin and nose were distant beneath what was happening as he was lifted two feet off the ground and going even higher.

Then, through the agony . . .

He began to smile.

The chain clicked to a stop ten feet up as Mike slammed on the button again.

Howdy swayed in the air slightly, his lips wide in a grin, blood dripping from his mouth. Having confronted the pain.

"Carleton," Mike shouted, looking up at the now helpless monster. "Does it hurt?"

Howdy peered down and started slowly moving his feet. Making his body slowly sway from side to side, like he was on a swing. The hook digging through his muscle caused more pain, but Howdy was taking dominion over it.

"You know, Michael," he rasped from above as his body continued to swing left to right. "I bet Genevieve felt a lot like this . . . When . . . When I was inside her." Then laughter, unfiltered, unrepentant, roared out of him.

"No," Mike whispered as this additional horror flooded his mind. As image after image flashed in his mind, making everything so much worse.

His eyes searched the room, frantic.

Then he saw it. He darted toward the bar area.

"What are you going to do, Michael?" Howdy screamed. "*Arrest me?*"

Mike came back holding a half bottle of whiskey.

He pulled the cork off and splashed high over Howdy's chest, face, legs. soaking him as he swung by in wider and wider arcs.

"Fuck you!" Mike screamed in a blind rage.

Howdy stopped laughing as he caught a glance of Mike's eyes. At the intent behind the badge. And he looked . . . thankful.

Mike sneered. "What's the matter, Carleton?! Didn't think I would?"

Mike reached into his pocket and pulled out a book of matches.

"Well, guess what," Mike said. "You wish is finally coming fucking true."

He struck a match. Then lit the whole book.

"This is for Genevieve."

As Howdy swung by, Mike threw the flaming pack.

The arc of the matches was slow in both of their eyes. The seconds were stretched thin as time slowed.

The impact was perfect.

Fire erupted across Howdy's chest like a blossom. Flames spread up his shoulders, caught the hair on his arms, and lit his hair like dry paper. He thrashed wildly, screaming as the flames spread over him. He was in pain he could not control, but he welcomed it.

"Pain is a uniquely personal experience, Carleton!" Mike screamed. Unable to restrain his hate. Knowing he was giving Carleton Hendrick, Captain Howdy, exactly what he had wanted.

As the chain swung close to the wall, Howdy's body

hit one of the thick curtains and immediately passed the flames, and the whole curtain was engulfed. The flaming whiskey also dripped off his body, landing on the dust sheets that covered all the tables, catching them alight.

Mike staggered back, barely avoiding the flamed that was starting to surround him. He moved to the other side of the room, shocked as Howdy's burning frame contorted, swinging back and forth, screaming like an injured animal.

The fire spread quickly over him and soon turned orange, then red, then black. Then there was nothing more from the monster. His body swung, charred and still burning. A burning mass against the brightly flaming room around him.

The fire soon spread upward. Every bit of fabric had caught onto the inferno and started to roar. Soon, the fire began to catch onto the wooden beams on the ceiling, spreading across it like a wave.

"*Mike!*" came a cry.

Mike turned, teeth bared, ready to strike, still in a rageful fugue.

"Hey, it's me," Steve said, hands raised.

The recognition sank in.

Mike glanced back into the burning room, at the suspended body.

"Come on, we've gotta go!" Steve shouted urgently, grabbing Mike by the arm. Turning him.

The winch creaked from the other side of the room, followed by a loud thud.

As they both looked back to the flaming dance

floor. Neither Mike nor Steve could not fathom the blur of movement that screamed toward him.

Captain Howdy.

Blackened. Burned.

One arm outstretched, he grasped toward Mike in violent desperation, with his shoulder split in two from below the bone, the hook having ripped straight through, spurting blood out as he roared furiously across the room.

Above, the wood on the ceiling began to crack as the fire ate into it.

Below the freight train of still burning flesh and murderous intent somehow still breathing and upright, came at them with insurmountable strength.

Mike stood motionless, unable to react.

Steve, though, managed to grab his partner just in time. He pulled them both clear as Howdy's flaming hand swung through the air, missing Mike's face by a fraction of an inch. Steve then kicked out at this burning force, knocking Howdy back into the middle of the room.

With a sudden crash, one that sounded like a forest falling, the ceiling quickly buckled inward. The aged, fragile beams had quickly lost their fight against the fire.

Howdy glared at them both. "Kill me!"

Before he could advance again, a torrential downpour of burning beams and slate slammed down from above, crushing him in an instant.

. . .

From outside, smoke bled from every crack of the old church as a large column of gray spiraled up into the sky, entwined with the rising flames that burned within.

In the distance, sirens grew louder as they approached.

As the first cruisers pulled up, the doors of Xibalba were flung open.

Mike and Steve came stumbling out, coughing, covered in ash.

EPILOGUE

I t was almost 3 a.m. as Mike Gage sat in the
hallway just outside his daughter's room, the tip of
a cigarette smoldering in his fingers. He hadn't
smoked for many years, but that night, he had lit one
just to feel something familiar.

It had started so slowly yet ended so quickly when
the ceiling of Xibalba came down. That was it. Carleton
Hendricks, Captain Howdy, did not rise out of the
rubble like some kind of immortal beast, even though
Mike would have not been surprised if he had. No. He
was dead. His body had been recovered. Crushed into
pulp. Only the metal piercings over his body had been
left unbroken.

And now it was all over and had been for many
weeks.

Toni was asleep in their bedroom. At least their
marriage seemed to be getting better, bit by bit. Gone

were the snide comments, but there was still a long, long way to go for them to be anywhere near fixed.

As for Genevieve, she hadn't spoken much since she had been rescued. A few words here and there. "I'm tired." "I'm not hungry." "Can I just go to bed?" She hadn't said much more. She hadn't even cried since she got out of the hospital. But she had screamed. Every night, she had screamed. And that night was no different.

He had just left her room, after holding her, telling her it was all okay. Finally, she had drifted back to sleep, and he sat there, in the hallway, wide awake and trying to piece together all that had happened, just like he did every night.

He had asked her *that* question a few days ago. "Did he touch you? More than the needles? You can tell me, you know." Since Captain Howdy had shouted down to him from the hook of what else he did to Gen, it tore him apart inside.

But she hadn't flinched at the question. She'd just looked back, still and calm, and said, "It's okay."

That was all. That was everything.

And the silence meant more than her words ever could.

Because if it were true, if Carleton Hendricks had done as he said, what then? What did that mean for her? She didn't show any signs of pregnancy, but that didn't mean she couldn't be . . . And what about diseases? What of her mind? She was violated on the outside but on the inside, too? If it was true, there was no part of her that Howdy didn't destroy.

Mike needed her to be safe, to be happy but after what happened, he had no idea what he could do. He thought he made her safe before, but she was taken. Again. And though Howdy was dead, there was still so many dangers out there.

He stubbed the cigarette out on the floor, not caring about the mark it would leave on the wood, then leaned back against the wall. His head thudded against it softly as he closed his eyes.

Was Hendricks insane? Sure. Deluded? Definitely. But . . . evil?

Mike had spent twenty years trying to believe that evil was not real and was just circumstance plus illness plus desperation wrapped up in some variation of bad biology. That if you unpeeled the layers enough, you'd find the damage. The logic. The cause. The switch that had been flipped one too many times. He believed that evil was just an easy excuse. But . . . after what he had seen, he could not see what Hendricks did as anything but evil. But the thing that really gnawed at Mike . . . was who was to blame. Who created the evil? After all, Victor Frankenstein was the true monster, not the thing he built.

Sure, Hendricks had that switch, and he did unspeakable things the first time around. Was that his fault? The hospital didn't think so. The jury didn't think so. They saw it as childhood trauma manifesting. One that could be cured.

Mike had read the reports on Hendrick's years in the psychiatric facility. He had been on suicide watch most of his time there before he finally accepted the things he had done and moved on from his self-destructive guilt. He had tried to find God, tried to make amends with his own shattered soul. Hated what he was. Hated what created him. Wanted to make good with the world.

But what came next . . . What he did . . .

There was no doubt about what happened. He didn't snap of his own accord. He was pushed off the edge, and Mike could have stopped it. Stopped the mob from taking him away. If he had, would Howdy still be just a bad memory that Carleton Hendricks medicated away? Would the evil inside still be safely locked in its cage?

After all that, all Mike could console himself with was Genevieve. She had survived. But something in her eyes, just beneath the surface, said she was beyond his repair. He wondered if this was her switch into something else. He could not help but wonder if Hendricks had planted a seed and simply walked away. A piece of him, rotting quietly under her skin.

No. I can't think like that.

Or maybe . . . Maybe this was all just what Hendricks wanted. He wanted Mike to doubt. That the vile thing he said was not a physical torture but a mental one. A final act of cruelty. The switch that would push him to kill Howdy. Something Howdy maybe could not do himself.

Genevieve's door opened, and Mike opened his eyes.

She stood there in the soft spill of hallway light, hair tangled, an oversized hoodie hanging off her. She looked down at her father before sitting on the floor beside him without a word. Without looking at him.

He didn't know if she'd ever tell him what really happened.

But that night, she came out.

And maybe that was enough.

He'd be right there for her, that night, the day after, always.

And in that moment, he knew, she would be there for him, too.